Th

MW00415704

"*The Circle That Fits* is a tender Bildungsroman that traverses the ligatures between destiny and identity. Daniel is both hungry for his parents' love, and maimed by its yoke—unable to be without them and unable to be free of them. I found myself in Daniel, adroitly told through Kevin Lichty's graceful and sincere prose. Tremendously crushing yet lilting with hope, *The Circle That Fits* will take you into dark and mystical corners of carny life from the perspective of a boy who allows us to witness exquisite love through the grotesque. This is a novella I didn't know I needed, and one I now can't imagine being without. Lichty has given us an astounding treasure."

— Kalani Pickhart, author of *I Will Die in a Foreign Land*

"At the heart of Kevin Lichty's *The Circle That Fits* are two spectacles: the public display of a traveling carnival's thrills and the private drama of a fracturing family's pain, neither of which can exist apart from the other, at least not for our young protagonist. Lichty renders both his worlds with precise, surprising language and an enviably moving surrealism, one grounded always in the rich emotions running through this gripping novella."

— Matt Bell, author of *Appleseed*

THE

CIRCLE

THAT

FITS

Kevin Lichty

INDEObjectENDENTLY PUBLISHED BY
DRIFTWOOD PRESS

Independently published by Driftwood Press
in the United States of America.

Managing Fiction Editor: James McNulty
Assistant Editor: Stephen Hundley
Readers: Claire Agnes & Dan Leach
Cover Image & Interior Images: formyths
Cover Design: Sally Franckowiak & James McNulty
Interior Design & Copyeditor: James McNulty
Interior Image Design: Jerrod Schwarz
Copyeditor: Jessica Holbert
Fonts: Bembo, Sitka, Garamond, Balboa,
& Merriweather

First published on October 25th, 2022
ISBN-13: 978-1-949065-18-3

Please visit our website at www.driftwoodpress.com
or email us at editor@driftwoodpress.net.

Most people think you start with a circle; close the space off so you can create inside of it, but Dad said starting with a circle is a mistake. A circle collapses without the scaffold of the eight to hold it together, and without the eight, everything becomes chaos. Dad said you begin with a figure eight, because a figure eight outlines the potential space that might exist. A circle comes second; define your borders, Dad said. He poured quickly, from the wrist, but carefully. Without care, he said, you'll get wild arms flying everywhere, a mess.

When Mom was here, she had helped. She'd stand behind Dad and whisk the powder into batter, their two backs pressed against each other. Sometimes I had to crawl between their legs to get from one side of the trailer to the other. At night, she helped me catch fireflies in the fields when it was warm enough, taught me how to cup them in my hands so they would illuminate the spaces between my fingers. We'd sing a song to them, blow into the hollow of our hands and let them go.

Most nights we found Dad sleeping under the foldaway table when we got home. Mom said he slept that way because he spent three years running away from monsters who wanted to eat him in the jungle, and when he had come home he thought he'd be safe, but he found monsters here too.

Sometimes, Mom and me would make a circle with our arms and we'd spin and spin until I lifted off the ground, and I would fly around the circle of our bodies and feel the world pulling at my feet, trying to pull me away, but Mom held on so tight.

When Dad finished with a funnel cake, he would fish it out of the fryer with a pair of tongs and let it drain before releasing it onto the plate in my outstretched arms. He started to let me powder them when I was seven, and I remembered then that on a clear day when the sun shone in through the front windows, the powdered sugar had looked like stars falling through the cylinder.

One day, my mom let go. I remember it like a release, like I was unstuck and floating free of everything until I fell to the ground and all the wind was knocked out of me. I laid there in the grass for a long time, heaving, waiting for Mom to come rushing over and pick me up. I watched an ant crawl across my arm in circles, its antennae waving. After a while, I stood up and looked around and she was gone. Dad said he didn't know what had happened to her, told me that the best thing to do is to just draw a circle around my heart and close it in. Here, he said, giving me a funnel. He dragged a stool over to the two fryers, looked me in the eye and patted it. The first thing you have to do is make an eight.

People came to watch my dad create. He was a calligrapher. They came to the windows and watched him funnel out galaxies into the oil, his wrist light as air. What he created was both crisp and soft. Most people said it melted on their tongues, almost as if nothing was ever there. My dad said it's because he pays more attention to the spaces in-between rather than where he's been pouring. He said people don't understand this because most people think a circle comes first, but a circle comes second.

Dad said our trailer wasn't big enough to hold hope. We need the room, he said. We were getting rid of Mom's things, grabbing armfuls of clothes and stuffing them into black trash bags. We pulled out the bins of her lipsticks, her body spray, her shampoo. Here, the book she was reading before she left—dog-eared, spine broken in five places, corners of the cover torn away. Here, the bin of her headbands and hair clips to hold back her mass of curls from her face. I took out a clasp: square, pewter-colored, covered in rhinestones.

I remember the last time she wore it. It was a Saturday, my eighth birthday. The carnival was open late. She'd said, come on, we're going to be like everyone else tonight. We stepped out of the trailer into the cool together, her hand wrapped around my hand, breathed air thick with the smell of fry oil.

We walked through the midway. The clasp in her hair absorbing all the reds and yellows and blues.

What do you want to eat? she asked.

We walked past everything that was fried—the french fries, the corn dogs, the chicken, the egg rolls, the onion rings, the fried ice cream, the elephant ears, the fried Oreos and Twinkies and candy bars.

Bob's kabobs, I said. His open fire, his skewers of meat, his black char on the peppers. We watched Bob slap the skewers onto the fire, the juice drip down onto the wood, heard it pop, watched the curl of black smoke rise into the sky, watched him turn and turn and turn.

And lemonade, I said. The kind made by hand. We watched the floating hemisphere of a lemon be pressed into a glass, its clear juice leak in the sugar—white, translucent, gone.

We sat under a canopy strung with incandescent lights and ate. She bought me a caramel apple embedded with peanuts and we walked to the games and she let me throw darts at balloons, my favorite. Jason gave me the real darts because it was my birthday. I felt the heft of them in my hand. They felt heavy and deadly and beautiful. I won a fuzzy lion hand puppet and a Harley Davidson keychain. Mom told me to hold on to that keychain, hold on to it tight.

Someday we're going to have a key to put it on and a door that will fit it and you'll have your own bed to sleep in, the same one every night, in the same place. And you'll have the same grass to play on, and the same friends to play with, and they'll come over and we'll have water fights in the afternoon and have cookouts and make popsicles out of orange juice and toothpicks, and Dad will come home from work and we'll sit down at a table and eat roasted chicken with fried potatoes every night and I'll put you to bed and tuck you in and everything will be the same in the morning.

What about the Ferris wheel? I said.

You love the Ferris wheel, don't you?

It's my favorite.

Come on, she said.

And we went and got into the bucket and held on to the arm bar and rocked as it went higher. We reached the top and Joe Joe held us up there so I could look out at the black mass of trees down below, see the road snake away, see the cars moving back and forth, the circles of their lights, the orange haze from the town's streetlights rising into the black of the sky.

Here: Mom, the tangle of her hair pulled back, the clasp she wore shining white in the light of the Ferris wheel. Down below: the yellow of our Funnel Cake sign, the white pouring out from the front windows, the shadow of Dad moving left to right. I wanted to say something about the space between there and here, between the shadow of Dad and the light in Mom's hair, but I didn't know the words. Instead: the top, or near the top, of the Ferris wheel, the dark of the sky, the light on my skin yellow and white, the non-space between Mom and me.

Just like everyone else? I asked.

Just like everyone else, she said.

Then the Ferris wheel lurched, and for a moment, as the bucket swung out, I couldn't tell if we were still rising toward the sky or falling back to the earth.

Dad came out of the trailer and wheeled out the hand-cart. He stacked the bins one by one until the handcart was full.

Put that clasp in the bag, too, he said.

I'm going to keep this one.

There's no room.

I can put it in my pocket, I said. I put the clasp in my pocket.

That's not how this works.

But I don't have anything else, I said.

What did I tell you? He crouched all the way to his knees. His knees indented the loose dirt beneath him. Come here, he said.

I crouched down, too.

Draw a circle, he said.

We drew until the circles touched each other.

Now stand inside, he said.

I stood inside my circle and he stood inside his circle.

This is all the room you have now, he said.

But it fits in the circle with me, I said. I held the clasp in the palm of my hand.

He slapped my hand and the clasp flew up and burned in the orange shaft of the arc lamps and then fell into the dust. Everything outside of this circle doesn't belong, he said. And then he said, now put the clasp into that bag.

I walked over and picked the clasp up. I held it in my palm, felt the heft of it. It felt heavy and deadly and beautiful there. The rhinestones were prisms through my tears. I put it in the bag.

Now grab those other trash bags and that's all of it, he said.

Every year, we peeled off from the carnival and went to Sugarloaf, an arts and crafts fair in Gaithersburg, somewhere between Meyersdale and Winchester. Mom made us go. She said she needed a break, needed quiet, needed to walk the stalls and look at the carvings and smell the oils and drink the teas and try the honeys and to sit in the chairs that float and spin and hold you tight. And to just *be*, she said. Just *to be*. And so we went every year. Even after Mom left, we continued to go. Dad said it was because Sugarloaf was part of our circle now and the circle couldn't be broken once it's closed.

We made gallons and gallons of fruit punch, soaked the fruit overnight and pressed it through a sieve. And we folded pumpkin into our batter and sliced strawberries for toppings. Dad said we had to be artisans here. Here, it is about showing off, he said.

There was magic, too. There were marionettes who came alive and told stories, who sometimes invited us on stage so we could scowl at the moon and howl into the wind or skulk back to our caves, and when I howled into the wind, my voice carried past the walls of the warehouse. Afterward, a Willow sold unicorn blessings, and a line would form, and she would press a unicorn horn into the palm of their hands and bend down and whisper into their ear, and when she was done they cradled their hands as they walked away and stared down into it as if something was placed underneath their skin. And there was a wandering tree that moved through the booths. And when he swung his long limbs, they scraped against the concrete floor. And when he turned his head, his leaves would rustle and make music. And when he put his arm around you to take a picture, his stick fingers curled around your shoulders and pulled you in to his trunk, which was soft and squished and felt so unlike the bark of the trees outside.

One day, I saw the empty husk of the tree leaned against the bathroom wall. A man, red-faced and sweating, stood at the bathroom sink washing his face. I learned his name was Daniel, like me. And I learned he traveled, like I did, only in a different orbit.

I've seen you at all the shows, he said.

We come here every year.

I know. I know your mom and dad.

Oh, I said.

Your dad thinks I'm simple, but do you want to know a trick? he said.

What?

And he said your father thinks I'm simple because I live in a fantasy, because when I am out there I am not myself but something else. But no matter what happens out there, you never have to worry, because when it gets too hard, you can always escape up here. He pointed to his head.

And I thought about Dad at night and how sometimes I could hear Mom whispering him back to quiet, and how sometimes I was too afraid to move from underneath my blankets when Dad got up at night, and how sometimes Mom would send me to the outside bathrooms to wash my face and get a soda from the vending machines, and I wondered if escape meant the same thing all of the time.

Never forget what I said and you will be okay no matter what, Daniel told me. And he lifted the costume from against the wall and stepped inside and folded himself back into a tree and opened the door and ambled out into the crowd.

That same day I was picked out of the audience to be part of the show. And even after I saw the husk of the tree leaned against the wall of the bathroom, even after I saw Daniel, red-faced and sweating, standing at the sink, I pulled and pulled air into my chest and screamed as loud as I could.

Llewellyn, the pony ride man, used to let me feed his ponies sugar cubes in the purple darkness before the sun came up, the velvet of their lips curling around my fingertips as they pulled the cubes into their mouths and crunched. He told me the lips of a pony were like the lips of a woman. And when I said my mom's lips weren't like theirs, he said, not those lips, you idiot.

He once said to me that his ponies were the freest ponies in the entire world. I said to him, but they're yoked and have to walk around the same circle all day long with kids strapped on their backs, and he said they are free because they are yoked. He said, they are free because their entire world is that little circle in the ground and those kids. He said, they don't have to think about anything else besides that world, and in that world they are free.

He showed me how the basketball rims were bent to look straight, and how the milk bottles were unbalanced so they would never fall at the same time, and where the teenage girls gathered behind the arcade tent and pressed their bodies against the men who wandered to them. The only thing the man wants to do is to take and take and take, he said. I asked him who the man was and he told me everyone is the man.

So are you the man? I asked him.

Yes, he said.

Llewellyn was a wise man. He was the first one to tell me I didn't need to be a carny, that there was more to this world than asphalt and dirt and fried food and lights and vomit. He said my dad did what he did because he didn't know how to do anything else, said it was because he couldn't do anything else, because he couldn't exist anywhere else, because no one wanted him to. He said, is that how you want to be?

I said, why not?

He turned my head and said, look at those ponies one more time.

Asphalt was the river we traversed, oil-slicked, polluted with drive-thru fast food wrappers, convenience store beer cans, truck stop condoms. But sometimes it was also the island we lived on too. Candied and slick with drool and vomit and dust, we made our home there for a week or two. Digging into the asphalt was impossible, so we floated our homes above it, padded our floors with old towels, blankets, furs, old insulation ripped from derelict homes along the side of the highway, egg crate foam. Every morning we woke up together as one, as if it were planned, as if we were a collective, a hive moving to the same internal clock of the carnival. Fuck that, most of us would say. We got up and saw the sun smear across the horizon, a dandelion bloom in the cracks of the asphalt, a grasshopper land on our shoe. Home was here and here and here and here.

I remember the day Joe Joe lost his hand. Joe Joe had been trying to repair the motor on the Ferris wheel, jamming his entire body against the torque wrench, his face chord-strained, his body quivering behind the metal, when he slipped. Knuckling under, his arm flung out and wedged itself between the teethed gears when the motor bellowed, coughed, ground to a start, eating Joe Joe's hand to the wrist.

Listing to the side, he ripped himself free, hand separating from wrist, skin and muscle and bone, like a zipper. Meat hung from the stump, then the blood, overflowing the fingers wrapped around the wrist, poured out onto his chest inking the flannel red, a wail escaping from his eyes like the eyes of prey, like the realization that the talons have sunk in, severed your back without warning.

Near me, Llewellyn pushed through the crowd, ran to Joe Joe, wrapped a towel around his wrist, cinched it with a leather strap and pulled tight.

Okay, don't look at it, look at me, Llewellyn said.

People surrounded them, made a ring of them, but all that did was create a stage with Joe Joe and Llewellyn at its center.

Quiet down, the people told each other.

Re-cinching the leather strap, Llewellyn picked me out of the audience, told me to get more towels. So I went to his trailer, gathered a pile of them into my hands, ran back and gave them to Llewellyn, who undid the cinch, replaced the soaked towel with a fresh one, and pulled the strap tight around Joe Joe's wrist again.

Taking the saturated towel from the ground, I ran and ran, felt the weight of the blood, felt the blood seep onto my hands, pour down my arms like cords of rope, felt Joe Joe's blood flake off my elbows as I ran like a melting ice cream cone, felt my heart pumping my blood, my blood safe inside still, safe and whole and still bringing oxygen to my hands which held Joe Joe's blood-soaked towel that I held out in front of me like a giblet sack, like an urn.

Under a tree by the Casselman, I dropped to my knees,

lowered the towel into the current, watched the blood get pulled from it. Viscous cords of coagulate clung to the fibers, danced in the eddies of the river. Water flowed over my wrists, cooled the blood in my hands. Xanthic pedals of honeysuckle and dandelion and marigold floated down the river, coated my arms. Yoked to me, I heard the ripping sound of Joe Joe's hand echo in my ears. Zephyr winds blew a yellow haze of pollen over the river.

My world was the smell of hot oil and fried batter and powdered sugar, the heat from the fryers and our bodies trapped by the small metal walls of the trailer, the windows where people waited for me to pass my world to them on paper plates for $2.75, pass through the window into the darkness and colored lights and roar and music, pass to people whose eyes had become the size of Ferris wheels, their squeals still imprinted onto the corners of their mouths. Outside, in the darkness, I could see them expanding and expanding; inside, I had to stay small to fit into the space my father had given me.

After the lights had gone out, after the people had popped and liquefied and had gone home, we tore down under the yellow arc lamps of the 4H barn with powdered sugar stuck to our aprons like gum, the smell of Murphy's oil soap and earth and cooking oil, the blackened ends of funnel cake embedded in our fingernails.

When it got busy—days gray and cold where people came for our plates that warmed their hands, for our fried dough that radiated from the belly—we would run out of supplies and Dad would send me with a list and a hundred dollars in ones and fives from the till. This was my landscape.

On the way back one day, bags of baking powder and flour in my arms, I found a redheaded boy crouched in the shade between a station wagon and a minivan, his knees coated in mud, his cheeks crimson and splotched with freckles.

Hi, he said.

Hi, I said.

Want to see my Transformers? he asked.

What are those?

And he opened the minivan door and reached in and pulled out two giant robots with translucent wings and skin that changed colors in the light.

They're prehistoric, he said.

I dropped my bags and crouched down next to him and we stomped through the prehistoric mud swamps of an alien planet; our robots transformed into ancient bugs gliding over the quicksand and mud and ooze and attacked each other.

Why aren't you at the carnival? I asked.

I got sick on the Ferris wheel, he said.

Oh, I said.

I attacked him from above, dive-bombing from the hood of the station wagon. Our robots crashed together and fell into the mud, sunk down into the cool, wet earth, drowned. We made drowning noises. A laser baked the earth dry and we were free.

The guy wouldn't stop the ride, he said. It kept going around and around and I didn't think it was going to stop and I just got nervous. I'm not a baby.

That's Joe Joe, I said. He's an asshole.

I'm not a baby, he said. I just get nervous sometimes.

I do, too.

We flew our robots around the minivan, chasing each other in the coolness of the shadow, expanding and expanding until our bodies were the size of planets, our circles the size of orbits around the sun. The wind and the sun and the shadow. Us, breathless, out of breath, collapsing into the mud.

I wanted to know what school was like. And he told me it was mostly being still and lining up single-file with fingers over your lips, or quietly sitting crisscross applesauce to listen to stories during library days.

What's crisscross applesauce?

He sat down in the mud Indian style.

Oh, I said.

What's being in the carnival like? he asked.

And I told him that Llewellyn told me I was free because my world was so small and in that smallness I was free to be as big as I wanted to be, but inside everything was too bright.

Sometimes when I'd finished closing, I walked across to help Llewellyn get the horses down at night. I walked across the midway and through the rides, through the scaffolds of their bodies, tentacled and quivering and inert. And when I saw the Ferris wheel silhouetted blacker against the black of the sky, I knew to turn right out past the circular rut of the pony rides to the stables because even in the dark the Ferris wheel was at the center. And if there weren't stables on the fairgrounds, sometimes Llewellyn had to stable the horses in his traveling trailer and double them up.

When I would get there, Llewellyn always had the horses dressed down and washed and was brushing them, a can of beer in his hand. He always had something to say. I could always see it written on his mouth.

If you close your eyes and forget, the circular motion will almost feel like progress, Llewellyn told me. He tipped the can to his lips, drained it, threw the can into a bag next to his cooler, opened another, tipped his head back and drank again.

I grabbed a brush and rolled the steam off M&M's body with the bristles and she stopped bucking her head and stood still and quiet. Llewellyn bent down and lifted her hoof and scraped the mud off her shoe and the mud fell down into the hay.

And I asked him, what are you talking about?

And he said, did you ever notice every single ride here runs in circles?

And I said, but those are just rides.

And he said, are they?

And I said, yeah, we're different.

And he said, are we?

And he crouched down into the dust and moved aside some hay and began drawing in the dirt. And he said, we're here right now. And this is 95 right here. And he traced his finger down. And he said, by December we'll be in Jacksonville, and by January we'll be in Ocala, then Sarasota, then Tampa. And he drew his arm back up and said, by May we'll be again in Chesterbrook, and in September we'll be here again right where we are right now.

Now what does that look like to you?

A circle, I said.

M&M has a lot of tangles in her mane tonight. Make sure you get them all out, he said.

And he reached down into the cooler, into the ice, dug and dug, found another can and tipped it to his lips.

He said, without the blinders, sometimes it's hard to forget. You get that eye rolling out into the world looking around. You need to watch yourself. Look what's right in front of you and forget everything else.

And I thought of Mom letting go of me. I thought of her clasp that I couldn't let go of. I thought of Dad under the table, probably, right now in the dark curled into his nightmares. I thought of Llewellyn's horses and how sometimes, when he took the blinders off, they stopped moving.

Llewellyn pushed a can into my hand, still shedding the ice water from the cooler. And he said, now drink this beer and go home.

Llewellyn tried to sell Princess to me, said she was too good, too proud, too strong to be a pony ride pony.

Look here: this red ribbon she won down in Winchester last month. Look here: the snowflake pattern. Look here: the neck, long and lean and inclined. Look here: the forelegs, square and true. He said she deserved to be in a stable eating carrots, brushed and braided and given collars of dandelions to eat.

I wanted to be too good to be a change-man, too good to be kneeling in the dirt and loosening the bolts of the funnel cake sign with my fingertips in the dark, a flashlight pinned between my neck and shoulder so I could see, wanted to be stabled and fed carrots and dandelions, brushed and braided, win ribbons for my perfect canter.

He said, give her a ride, you know, a quicksie, you know, like one of those speed dating deals.

Llewellyn had no saddle that fit her, nor bit and bridle that suited her, and so I straddled her bareback, held between my hands a braided rope.

Give her a looksee, Llewellyn said. Just kick them heels into her ribs and she'll git.

So I did. And she fired the cannons of her legs down

the mud and gravel path between the haunted house and the trailers, the braided rope a redhot friction, down past the Ferris wheel, the hurricane, the Superloop, her body a universe I had to cling to, cling to or be thrown into the void of her absence. And so I clung to the blur of her, her rippling undulating mass. I loved her.

The negotiations continued all day, the sun giving way to the red and blue and white of the carnival, the stars below obliterating stars in the sky. But I was twelve, and the negotiations were really between the pony ride man and Dad, and Dad had no intention of feeding Princess carrots or making collars of dandelions or braiding her hair.

But I wonder, now, if things would have been different if Princess didn't have to sling kids every day, chained to the rusty spokes of Llewellyn's pony ride. Would Princess wear perpetual fear in her eyes? Would her snowflakes have become dust? Would the five-year-old girl still be sprawled on the ground with her skull crushed and her blonde hair caked in candy apple and blood? Would Llewellyn still be raising his rifle to her head if Dad had dreamed like I had?

We found Llewellyn wedged under the ticket booth counter, a needle still in his arm, staring at a painted boy clutching the balloon in one hand and the androgynous disembodied hand of a mother-father in the other. In the greasy red-blue light of police cars along the side of I-70 somewhere between Frederick and Ellicott City, the coroner told us it was an overdose of his insulin, that he had injected himself at least five times in the same place, that the massive dose most likely caused him to lose consciousness without much pain, that he slipped into death without much fuss, without a word or a note or a reason.

But we all knew what he wanted, knew it because he had hitched a ride from Meyersdale halfway to Lansdowne, hitched it on the ticket booth, stowing away on the eternal road, gateway, communal bank, hitched that ride because he wanted to ride with us, stay with us. It was not us he was running away from.

So we convinced Rolfe, the lion handler and taxidermist, to remake Llewellyn as we remembered him, so that he could remain with us, sit and visit with us, still share a beer in the circled trailers after hours with us, the heat of a bonfire to his back crisping the hair on his neck.

He is not a pet, a hunt-kill to mount and display and gaze at, Rolfe said.

It is his wish, we replied. Can you not see the intent, the inherent request in his actions?

He is not decoration, Rolfe said.

No. He is the Ferris wheel, the carousel, the strength tester. He belongs with us.

Let me get my tools, Rolfe said.

So he stayed with us through Lansdowne and Winchester and Shenandoah, took his turn in the arcade, the fairway, watched over our campsite in the night, the marbles of his eyes burning in the bonfire.

Much later, the police would find the ponies hidden in the brush along the banks of the Casselman behind the fairground, M&M and Jinx and Rascal and Daisy, each shot a single time. How he had dragged all four horses into their hiding places, the police didn't know. How he fired four rounds without anyone noticing, without spooking the horses, they didn't know. No one could recreate the moment for us, their deaths, and so we were free to imagine that he shot them in their sleep, without tether, so that they couldn't see their brother, their sister before them shot one by one, so that they didn't bare their teeth, so that their breath did not steam with fear in the cold night air. We dreamed that Llewellyn cradled each of their heads in his hands, that he cried for what he thought he must do, that he caressed each of them into death, whispered them into oblivion, that it was quiet and soft and reverent.

For five dollars, Rolfe took pictures of families with his lion—pictures of smiling children sitting dangerously close to the lion's mouth, pictures of girls hugging the lion's mane, pictures of boys petting the lion's back, pictures of twins with the lion's massive paws covering their laps or heads or chests as they lay beneath the lion with their tongues lolling out and their eyes rolled back and their arms thrown over the platform dramatically, pictures of parents whose eyes resembled those of a gazelle staring into wheat-colored grass that swayed in the early morning breeze. Pictures of the lion staring back.

I liked to watch Rolfe with the lion, how quiet and still they both were. I used to watch him hold the lion's stare, hold his arm out palm downward, always downward, how he moved like his body wasn't pulled down by gravity, like his muscles floated in liquid. I used to watch that dance: the thick chain around the lion's neck scraping across the platform as Rolfe moved and the lion's head followed. Rolfe said the chain was for the parents, not for the lion.

Rolfe would not tell us where the lion came from, so we made a history: Rolfe had been a lion tamer's apprentice in a circus, and he watched every night as the ringleader's wife would go into the lion tamer's tent until the ringleader found out and poisoned the lion tamer's lions in revenge, all but one vomiting blood and bile and stomach until they died, or he'd been a zookeeper and stole the lion cub after its mother died in childbirth, or he'd been a merchant marine and bought the lion cub at a seller in a port of call and he smuggled it on board his ship and hid it in the machine room, fed it scraps from the kitchen, covered its piss in vinegar and disappeared with it in the first port of call he could.

Llewellyn said where the lion came from didn't matter, said the lion was always here and so always will be. Dad said the goddamn lion was a danger, said it was going to get the whole carnival shut down one day.

Rolfe sat down next to me one night right after Llewellyn had been found. He handed me a grape soda, turned to me and said, the lion just started following me one day.

That doesn't make any sense, I said.

And he said he used to be an animal control officer and got called in as backup one day to a job that was too big for the responding team. No one told him what was going on and when he got there the other officers were frozen on the back porch and he could hear the screams of a woman out somewhere in the wheat-colored grass. And he asked the three other officers what was going on, and they told him not to go out there, told him they used everything they had, but they couldn't touch him.

And Rolfe said he went out anyway, went out into all that swaying grass, and he followed the screams until he came upon a man and a woman and a lion. And the man's spine was broken and pulled away from his rib cage, and the woman was beneath the lion and the lion had his claws deep in her thigh and the jaws of his mouth were wrapped around her throat, and every time she screamed the lion tensed and its teeth pressed against the flesh of her neck.

And he said the lion was covered in blood—around his mouth, in his mane, on his chest. And he said the lion stared at him with those honey-colored eyes, moved them without moving his head and just held him there in those eyes, in those wheat-colored eyes.

What did you do? I asked.

And he said he removed his vest and his shirt and un-buckled his belt and let his pants falls to the ground. And then he removed his boots and his underwear and stood there naked with his arm out, palm downward. And then he said he closed his eyes and walked forward until he walked right into the lion, until he could feel the silk of the lion's pelt, feel the warmth of the lion's skin, until he buried his face in the lion's mane and then the lion let go and cried.

During the day, Dad began to harden and crust over, his back a vice grip that pulled his body over the funnel cake fryers into a C, a concentration. When he talked, he only said what we needed—more batter; more oil; powder this; change for a ten; change for a twenty. In this way, we were able to shrink the space between us, focus on need, on want, the job, the ache in our feet, the tightness of our backs, the people outside standing in their lines, their faces bathed in yellow, their hands cradling our plates. The days were easy—we knew what to do with our hands and our mouths—and if our bodies touched, they touched because they had to, because they had to move in those directions.

But at night, after everyone who had needed us left; after the colors of the midway were shut off, in the dark and small spaces that were left in our trailer, the hard shell Dad created during the day liquefied and softened. Sometimes, I'd wake up and he'd be under the table, curled around its single leg. Sometimes his eyes would be open in the shadows beneath the arc lights staring, the big blue circles of them looking into mine unseeing. In those moments, I was always someone else—Mom or Aunt Christa or Grandpa or some-one named Sergeant Brown. And in the universe of his wide blue eyes, I would get sucked into his dreams and nightmares and he would yell and scream, claw and grab and pull me into his chest and squeeze until I couldn't breathe.

I told Llewellyn once that Mom had told me he got this way because he was being chased by monsters in his sleep. Llewellyn said Mom was full of shit, said this wasn't about monsters, that monsters don't take that way, told me to remember it was *the man* who did.

Before, when it got bad, Llewellyn let me sleep with the horses. And I would lay on their straw and listen to their breath in the darkness and hear their hooves shuffle against the ground and watch the mass of their heads moving back and forth, up and down. And sometimes I would put a hand on their neck and push my face into the muscles and breathe them in, breathe in all of their energy and quiet and beauty; or I would put my hand over the soft part of their nose, the velvet of their lips, and close my eyes and match my breath to theirs and then sleep.

But Llewellyn was gone now, the straw and the shuffling and the breath, too—just Dad and me and his wide, staring eyes and his dreams in the dark.

I remember one night I woke up and went out to the common room and poured myself a glass of water and saw Dad under the table with his shirt pulled off and wrapped around his eyes. And I could see the heaving of his chest and his red and slicked skin. And I walked over to him and crouched down and held my hand out to his hot and wet skin, held my hand out towards him like he was a radiator to be warmed by. And he flinched, and I flinched, and our bodies jumped like two magnets fighting against each other.

He reached up to the shirt pulled around his eyes and pulled it tighter.

And he said, no, said no, please.

And I felt the heat of his body even on the other side of the trailer, the fever of his dream leaking out of him, burning him up, igniting him from the inside. And I remember this used to be Mom's job, to put her hand on his forehead.

So I crouched down and put my head under the table and held my hand out. And he flinched again, but I held my hand steady, held it out to his burning sleeping body and touched his shoulder. His body like a center of gravity. I fell into his orbit.

I pulled my hand away and saw the imprint of it on his skin, the white outline of my fingers. And he reached out and grabbed my hair and squeezed. He said, goddamn you motherfuckers. Is this it? Is this it? And he ripped at my hand and slammed my head against the ground and held it there, pressed me down like he was trying to push my head through the floor. And I squeezed my eyes shut and reached out and touched his forehead.

And he said, no. And he said, please.

And I fell into the cracks Dad made and was rooted.

It's okay, I said. It's okay, Dad. It's okay.

The next day he wouldn't remember, said he didn't re-member, but his body did. He pulled me closer, pulled me into his searing, red-hot orbit and asked me to promise him to never leave, said this is how it's meant to be right here, father and son, tradesmen, master and apprentice, like the ancients.

He picked up his funnel and said everything you need to

know pours out from this.

I said, okay, Dad. Can I go outside for a few minutes?

He said, sure.

I went outside and ran under a tree and in its shade I crouched down into the dirt and cupped an ant and pulled him into my hands. And the ant felt the map of my hands with its antennae. And I crouched down into the dirt again and picked up another ant, and another and another and another until my arms were covered in them and my skin burned with their stings.

I used to be mistaken for a girl. When Dad would take me with him to the bank or to get ice cream or pizza, everyone would always tell him how beautiful his daughter was. Sometimes he would correct them, sometimes he wouldn't. Even covered in soot and dust and grease, even covered in the red ink-blots of hot oil burns on my arms and neck, I was "beautiful." On the days Dad set me free, I could hear the mothers tell their sons to let the little girl go first.

It wasn't a problem until I turned eleven, when I had grown tall but not broad, when "beautiful" became "hot," when deference became aggression. Even after I grew hair on my legs, dark and curly and thick, I would hear people say, man, that girl has hairy legs. They would ask me why I didn't shave, ask me why I still had a flat chest. I could feel their hands on my ass, encircle my waist, their moist lips against my ear.

When we worked, Dad stared at me sideways, questing, seeing Mom's exaggerated features—her lips, her cheekbones, her curly hair. What did he see when he stared? I stared back with his eyes—lidded and defiant and angry. In this way, he saw himself in me, too, and was satisfied.

I learned to punch with Rolfe and Joe Joe and Dad by the firelight of the bonfire. Joe Joe crouched, circled around me, hooking me by the collar, spinning me around so that I became pinned into my shirt, exposed skin glowing in the fire. Short jabs to the ribs. Starbursts of pain. My body would tenderize, turn soft beneath his fist. I flailed back, entombed, blind. I learned to move as he moved, mirror his movement, stay away from his hook, protect my body. We made circles in the dirt. The purple of my ribs turned green, then yellow.

I got quick and hard, learned everywhere on the body that was soft and vulnerable and tender—under the armpit, just below the ribs on the right, below the sternum above the stomach, the throat, along the back just below the ribs to the right or left of the spine. Joe Joe showed them all to me, bent down with me in the dust as I heaved breath, said, do you see? You see.

Dad told me never to hit their face. Let them crumple and suck the dirt and walk away, he said.

Llewellyn watched from the perimeter, unblinking, with his marble eyes.

But Joe Joe was not the man who grabbed me in the dark of the arcade, who called to me from his pickup truck and said he wanted to eat my pussy, not the boys who made fun of my flat chest, my hairy legs. He was not the girl behind the ice cream counter who called me beautiful, who asked me if my hair was natural, who said I would have no problem attracting men when I got older and filled out, who said I'd know what an uncircumcised penis would look like one day.

The circles Joe Joe and I made were not the same as the grass I walked on during the day. The heat I felt dropping to the dust was not the same heat I felt when someone whispered to me that he wished I were older while his friends called jailbait. The light of the bonfire at night was not the same light that confused so many people. In the firelight I could be hard and quick, but outside I was tall but not broad.

Every year we went to Greenbelt for the Labor Day festival. Around midnight, we would spread out over an asphalt parking lot that was sandwiched between a police station and a community pool, erect the scaffolding of our lights so that on Friday morning the children and their adults and the adults of their adults could come and ride the hurricane and eat candy apples and funnel cakes and throw up on the Zipper and dunk their friends in the pool and kiss beneath the lights of the Ferris wheel and donate to the Maryland Democratic Party who sponsored the event and required a party worker to be present inside the booth of every station (five percent to the reelection committee). This meant that every year I worked from midnight to seven in the morning on Friday and then, covered in oil and grease and dust, with blood on my knuckles and knees, I would check in to the Holiday Inn. This was where I would stay on holiday for the holiday weekend, where I would eat potato skins from room service and swim in a pool already turning to ice and sit in a basement tanning salon and stare at the pictures of the tropical sun behind the counter and talk to the teenagers who worked there, who let me sit and talk for no reason, and look at the tanning beds like alien seed pods and watch movies in my room until Dad came home around one in the morning covered in the smell of the carnival. He would ask, how did your day go? And I would say, good. And we would eat cold pizza he brought back in a box gone translucent with grease, then fall asleep on the same bed.

I took my key from the front desk man, who stared sideways at his manager after I'd told him I forgot my key again, and carried my tiny suitcase up to whatever floor my room was on (the higher the better). In the room, I peeled off my clothes and threw them on the floor. And I turned on the air conditioner to high and stood in front of the window and looked down at the green belt of trees around the mall and the highway and the Denny's and the office building across from me and cooled the slick from my skin. And then I opened my tiny suitcase and found my bathing suit, the red one with the Superman symbol on the butt and put it on. And then in the secret pocket cut in the bottom of my suitcase I felt for the lace of a ribbon, pulled it out, unthreaded Mom's clasp, tiny and square and pewter and covered in rhinestones, and walked out of my room, took the elevator to the basement floor and stepped out—dark and beautiful and mine.

I padded across the concrete floor—past the laundry room, the pipes, the supply closet, up the stairs and out onto the pool deck, walked to the deep end, heard the water clack-clack against the skimmer. The air on my bare chest, already autumn chill, pulled the goose flesh out around my nipples. There was never anybody else there.

My ritual: I would hold Mom's clasp in my hand and

drop it down into the water and watch its distorted rhinestones shine in the deep and watch me back. I would stand on the "no diving" sign and breathe and breathe, dive in and kick my feet and down I went—the pop in my ears, the rough concrete bottom as I closed my fingers around the clasp and surfaced, heaving in a shivered chest of air. I would climb out and I throw it in again—dive, retrieve, surface. The water would pull me down, heavier each time. So I would throw it farther away, dive down longer, stay on the bottom longer, feel the mute of everything under the surface, the closeness of everything, hold the clasp in my hand and open my eyes and watched the surface ripple the sky above me.

I came up for air and a girl was standing on the edge of the pool watching. Her bleached hair. The curve of her hips. The space where her legs met the red of her suit.

You were down there a pretty long time, she said.

Yeah, I said.

What's your name?

Daniel, I said.

My name is Amy.

Hi, Amy.

You here by yourself?

I held up the clasp. The rhinestones glittered in the sun. I shook my head. My Mom, I said.

I was in the Holiday Inn when I got a phone call that wasn't for me, but still its ring woke me up, pulled me forward into the darkness, the snoring maw of Dad beside me, the hum of the air conditioner, the angry red light of the phone blinking.

Hello? I said.

Sorry to wake you so early, the voice on the other side said. I'm Sergeant Pilkington with the Green Belt Police Department. We're trying to get a hold of who we believe is your mother regarding a medical issue.

My mom? Do you know where she is?

Who is that? Dad said. His white arm reached out from the dark of the blankets.

No one, I said. Do you know where she is? I said into the phone.

That's why I'm calling you, sir.

Give me that thing. My father grabbed the phone, pulled it into the shadows of his face. Who is this? he said. No, that's not my son's mother, he said. No, that's not my mother either, he said. He handed me the phone. Hang it up, he said.

I put the phone back on the receiver. I felt the heat of

my father's back. I heard the hum of the air conditioner, on, even though the air had condensed on the window at night. Dad said it was because when you're in a hotel you take advantage of the air conditioner, turn it as low as it would go so you could carry it with you as long as possible once you were gone.

I went to the window, felt the cold of the air on my bare legs, looked down at the parking lot. The orange arc of the lights. The cars parked in front of Denny's, even then, at four in the morning. A car pulled in, parked; five people poured out. They seemed to dance in an invisible breeze below. I wondered who those people were and if they were like me: unrooted, having no address, no telephone, always moving, never stopping, shifting from one place to the next to the next—this week in Meyersdale, the next in Midlothian, the next in Culpeper—the names of the towns themselves invisible, anonymous, without place. I stared down into the yellow glow of the Denny's sign. Did they sleep in fields, in parking lots, in municipal campgrounds in a state park? Even now, with all the concrete in the world holding me here in this place, it didn't seem to matter.

Dad said if Mom wanted to contact me, she knew how. He said to make sure to keep that circle tight around my heart. Don't let anything leak out, he said. I buried my hands in flour and cornstarch and salt, carried fifty-pound sacks of mix over my shoulders to the truck every night, built calluses on my fingertips, salved the burns on my arms with lavender oil and beeswax, scraped the grease from fryers, worked until I smelled of funnel cake and sweat, Dad and I side by side, moving like twin bodies orbiting each other. We opened early. We closed late. The arms of our bodies hung low, the muscles of our shoulders no longer able to hold them away from the pull of the Earth. Now, I passed out as Dad passed out, into darkness, into an absence of time. Woke up before the sun, dragged our aching muscles into predawn.

Mom. Floating free of gravity. Like everyone else. A door and a key and a bed.

Where is Mom? I asked whenever we paused.

I don't know, Dad responded every time.

I believed him for a long time.

We set up. We broke down. We moved. In the convoy, I slept between towns. We moved north in the summer, south in the fall. In the winter, we toured Florida.

I found Mom's letter at a Laundromat outside Ocala, stuffed and crumpled in the laundry bag between the torn and faded folds of Dad's underwear. Dad was at the bar across the street having a beer. I was alone. I read it three times. She was living in an apartment in Harrisonburg. She worked as a food service manager at the university there. She wanted us to call her. I looked at the number written on the paper for a long time, gathered all the change I had and went over to the payphones and dialed.

Hello? a woman answered.

Mom?

Who is this?

It's me.

I don't have any children. You must have the wrong number.

Does Mrs. McCarthy live there?

Who?

Ellie.

I'm sorry, you've got the wrong number. The woman hung up.

I believed him for too long. I curled the letter into my fist, walked out of the laundromat and across the street and into the bar. I saw Dad, his back curled behind him, elbows propped on the bar, a glass of whiskey in his hand. He stared at the television screen, a baseball game on: spring training.

I walked over to him, held out my fist, said, did you want me to find this?

He turned, saw the paper. Where did you find that? he said.

How many more of them are there?

None. That's the only one she ever gave me.

I don't believe you.

Your mom gives up easy.

I thought of how many nights we had walked into the trailer and found Dad curled under the foldaway table, how many nights she had covered him in a blanket, how many nights she had cooled his sweaty brow with a damp cloth as he dreamed, how long she had put her back against his back in the funnel cake stand, how many years she had stayed on the road when all she wanted was a key and a door and a bed. I don't believe you, I said.

I slapped the glass out of his hand. You give up easy, I said. The glass flew, shattered against the floor.

Dad stood up, pushed me away with both arms. I fell backward.

Hey, take it easy there, someone down the bar said.

How many times have I told you not to let this happen? he said.

I stood up. Let what happen?

There's no room for hope, he said.

I held up my fist, shook the letter. This isn't hope. This is real.

That's a broken fucking promise.

Then I hit him, the soft spot just below the sternum, right above the stomach. I heard the air leak out of his mouth. He fell and heaved on the ground, spit. When he stood up, I saw in his eyes that he was no longer my father, no longer in the bar, no longer in Ocala. He feigned with his right at my temple, and when I raised my arms to protect my head, he landed another hit just below the armpit, and when I doubled over, he came across with his left and slammed his fist through my nose and then everything went blank. I felt him grab me by the collar and pull me close, felt him lift me off the ground. For a moment I was pulled completely free of gravity. Stars floated in the space in front of me. Blood and snot and tears curled around my mouth. And then I was either thrown to the ground or the ground was thrown to me and all the air was pushed out of my body and Dad was on top of me and I was curled in a ball and I felt the starbursts of his hands and fists and elbows all over me; and it wasn't even anger I saw in his eyes, it was loneliness; and it wasn't even me he was attacking—he was attacking past me, aiming his fists through my body toward a past I didn't understand. And he wasn't going to stop, and he wasn't going to stop, and Joe Joe hooked him by his collar, spun him around in his shirt, dragged him away from me and said, hey, man, what the fuck?

And I lay there on the ground, and my body was tenderized and full of ache. This is real, I said.

We came to Llewellyn in the darkness, in the ember glow of the bonfire. We came to him stumbling from our tents and trailers and trucks, pulled from our sleeping bags or beds. We came with offerings of fried chicken, elephant ears, cigarettes, PBR. And by the morning, a shrine had been constructed in the ash field at his feet. We came to him with our worries, our wishes, our dreams, our secrets, because in his rigid silence there was an opening inside of us, because inside the imprisonment of his body, we became free, because inside that freedom we were vulnerable, and in his glowing marble eyes, inside the actions he took, we saw ourselves, our potential selves—this was us staring toward a false sky; this was us along the banks of the Casselman; this was us staring and stiffening inside the ticket booth; this was us unable to stop moving. In this way, here was Llewellyn as mascot, as watchdog, as sentry. Llewellyn as curiosity, as attraction, as caller. Llewellyn as ticketer. Llewellyn as rumor, as myth. Llewellyn as tragedy. Llewellyn as cautionary tale, as signpost, as yard stick. Llewellyn as skeptic. Llewellyn as drinking buddy, as companion, as friend. Llewellyn as storyteller, as totem. Llewellyn as psychologist, as counselor, as guru, as priest.

And when I'd decided to leave, it was my turn to take that journey in the night, my face still swollen and purple and ugly, holding Mom's clasp in my cupped hands. The fire had burned down to smoke and ash. I laid her clasp at his feet, looked into the shadows of his face. I don't know what to do, I told him. I don't think I can stay here anymore. I don't think I can leave. I'm afraid of both.

There is more to this world than asphalt and dirt and fried food and lights and vomit, he said.

But I'm afraid of what will happen when I leave him behind.

All of his problems are man-made, he said.

But I don't know anything else.

Your Dad does what he does because he can't do anything else. You don't have to be a carny.

Llewellyn told me to go that night. He had always told me to go. Every day that we talked, his eyes wished for me a bigger universe, one that existed beyond the circle of the dirt and asphalt of our carnival.

Now, drink that beer and go, he said.

I found a beer warming by the fire and picked it up. Foam poured down the can. I tipped the can to my lips and drank and drank and felt its warm flat center pour down.

Thank you, I told Llewellyn.

The next morning, I walked to the fairgrounds before they awoke, before the caretakers and the artists and the chefs, before the ride operators, the ticket sellers, the barkers, before the gamesmen and singers and dancers, before the rides raised their great slumbering arms up, the scaffolds of their bodies up and up. I touched each one with my fingers, the vibrating cold cores of their engines. I moved through the midway, games, rides, the grandstand. I looped them twice. This was my vigil, my fire watch, my good-bye. The first sliver of sunrise burned the dew from the grass.

Others began to emerge from their tents, their trailers. I touched each one—hands, shoulders, back—the rough hue of their skin on my fingertips. They touched me back, passed bills to me in envelopes and pouches, ones and fives.

Rolfe came up to me, the lion on a chain beside him. The lion's claws dug into the dirt, seismic tremors, pulling out great clots of mud. He stared at me. I stared at him. Rolfe held out his hand, buried it within his mane, soft into soft, and the lion sat.

Rolfe pulled an envelope from his jacket and gave it to me, said to open it when I was ready. Said it's not what I think it is. Said if I wanted to go, go, but go now, because when Dad wakes up the going will be impossible. The lion's honey-colored eyes said Rolfe spoke the truth, said he always spoke the truth even when he was lying.

I put the envelope in my bag and walked out past the ticket booth, through the parking lot, over the hill and up to the road. There was Dad, sitting in the trailer with a cup of coffee cradled in his hands, his body held straight over the chair back. There was Mom, rising early in Harrisonburg and kneeling into her garden, the wet earth pooling around her knees. There was me, the weight of the backpack pulling me down, my boots double-tied tight around my ankles, the warm breath of morning on my skin, the crunch of my boots on the shoulder of the road to town. The first cars passed me and began to fill the parking lot. Behind me, Joe Joe spun the Ferris wheel into life.

Outside of the bus terminal, my bus to Richmond idling in front of me, I lie down and inhale the diesel and oil and tar and cigarettes. Before, I knew where the road would take me, the asphalt more like a string pulling me to the next place rather than a road of possibility. Already, our maps had been gridded and our plots had been established, and we knew where we had been and we knew where we were going and where we were before and before and before.

I lie down in front of the bus and see Dad filling the fryers with viscous white oil, turning the propane tanks on, the smell of the gas sharp and sour in his nose, watching the oil turn clear and slippery.

The bus doors open and people step over me and I close my eyes. Dad has not come to find me. Someone nudges my foot, says, you getting on? Says, can't fuck around with these guys, they'll leave you in a second.

I've never been to Harrisonburg. I don't know the map of the place. I don't know what Mom will be doing when I get there, what she has done, what she will do when I go to meet her, so I am free to imagine, free to dream on the ground in front of the bus. And so I see her in the morning with a newspaper, her body curved over the kitchen counter, resting on her elbows; and I see a window, where outside a tree, her tree, plays shadows across her face.

The bus driver steps over me, nudges me with his foot, says, you coming or what?

I open my eyes, stand up. My shirt is covered in black grease. I get on the bus, find a seat. The bus is half full. Everyone sits on their own row. Everyone hides behind the high backs of their chairs, folds down into their headphones and magazines. I've never been on a bus before.

The bus pulls out and the great black slick of the road stretches out into that possibility of unknowing. And the asphalt that used to hug me tight and hold me in my sleep as it pulled Dad and me to our next place unfurls and lets me go and my body feels unrooted, hurled and spun in the air.

And there is Dad propping open the shutters and hanging his sign. And there is Mom with a doughnut wrapped in paper leaving for work. And here I am sitting and watching the moving world with my hands in my lap.

With each new town, there is a stop and more people come onto the bus. We move up the peninsula in this way, slow and inviting, the door opening and opening. It takes seven hours to reach Jacksonville. There we wait and wait and they tell us we can get off the bus if we want to stretch our legs, but I sit still and watch the bus station from the window, all the other buses, all the other people moving in and out, sitting and standing and smoking and drinking. When we leave, our bus is full. And now the sun is low in the sky and it is getting dark and the carnival lights will be turning on and alive in the sunset and the screams and cheers of the riders will be heightened and more beautiful in the dark.

The woman sitting next to me asks, where are you going?

And I say to see my mom.

Isn't that nice. Where does she live?

I think in Harrisonburg.

You don't know?

I have this, I say. And I pull the envelope from my pocket and show it to her.

And she says that it was postmarked seven years ago and asks if this is all I have. And I say I see a tree and a yard and the shadow across her face in the morning. And she turns away from me, her whole body shrugging away, and she opens a bag of chips and crunches on them.

I turn and look out the window. The sun is almost gone now, a red smear across the bottom of the sky. I stare out into the world as the bus pushes into a stand of trees bracketing the road; and there is Dad doing both our jobs, moving back and forth between the window and the fryers, his hands pushing out through the window, passing the funnel cakes into the dark, his skin slicked and boiled and cast in shadow. And there is Mom, spooning fried potatoes onto a plate. And there is Llewellyn, his marble eyes lit by the fires, saying yes, saying go, saying go motherfucker go. And there is me, uncontained in my body, vibrating, staring out the front windows at the blade of world illuminated by the headlights of the bus.

Everywhere I go to find a job, for a place to stay, they want identification, two forms, a history—of payments, of work—phone numbers, people to call. I have none of these things. And because I have none of those things, they cannot help me. I go to the DMV, but they need a birth certificate to prove I am who I say I am, and when I tell them I don't know where I was born, the woman behind the counter tells me that's a problem, says, how am I supposed to know you are who you say you are? And I say, because I am standing here. And she says, that's not how it works. Says, until you come with proof, you don't exist to the state of Virginia.

In order to exist, I needed something fake, so I find a man who makes fake things. We meet in a photo kiosk in the parking lot of a K-Mart, his kiosk open after dark. Here, in this tiny box, he stands me before a white background and tells me what I need is an artist, someone who can craft the truth from a lie, says, this ain't no cut and paste job, says, it's going to cost you five-hundred for one good enough to fool who you need it to fool.

I don't have that much.

I can do half up front.

Half is all I have.

How can you put a price on your life? And he jabs the air between us with his thumb as if he could puncture his words into me.

I look around at the envelopes and envelopes folded into the alphabet cards. Blackened and bleached copies of photographs are tacked to the walls with notes of "don't do this" and "don't do this either" next to each. And there is Mom sitting in a living room chair with a photo album on her lap, asleep, her head tilted back against the chair back. There is Dad standing over a trash can, the embers of my photographs floating in the air.

Don't show any teeth, the kiosk man says. He takes my picture. He waits and takes two more.

If your card doesn't work, I'm coming to take my money back, I say.

Good luck with that.

We shake hands and I give him everything I have. Half my life passes into his. And he says, I can't hold on to this picture forever, all right? You don't get back to me in a month and I can't help you.

On days I work, I sleep in a motel, the kinds that don't ask for an ID or a deposit, and I shower and shave and trim my hair with a folding knife and lie down and stare at the ceiling and overhear the conversations of imaginary people whose lives begin and end in the symmetries between commercials. I lie in the bed and stare at the ceiling and let their lives wash over me; or sometimes I read whatever I can find—bibles, takeout menus, advertisements, emergency evacuation routes, shampoo directions, free newspapers found inside cages along the side of the road or at bus stops or outside of pharmacies.

On days I don't work, I go to Denny's and sit in a corner and order coffee and coffee and coffee and sit as long as the waitress will fill my cup. I find a waitress named Jewel who talks and smiles and pulls the strands of her hair up with pens. And I stare down into the black of my coffee, ripple the surface, watch the black bloom into cream. And Jewel asks what I see in there.

My universe, I tell her.

And she says, you're a strange cookie.

It's so small inside. Llewellyn used to tell me that the smaller the universe, the bigger I could be inside of it.

I never thought of it that way.

That's because it's bullshit.

You want more?

Always.

And in this way, inside the map of Jewel's section, I exist.

I overhear conversations here, too. The language: the slope of someone's back, the capillary pattern of their eyes. These men who sit at the bar and order their coffee black, their stacks of pancakes. Sometimes there are teenagers who come and talk close and fast and loud. Machine gun puffs on their cigarettes. The slurping of coffee. The drama of their lives animated and enormous—about "getting out," about "anywhere but here," about "hope," about "bullshit," about "despair." But everywhere is here, I want to tell them, and here is beautiful. Instead, I stir long streams of cream into my coffee and think of Dad in the morning with one hand on the small of his back, the other stretched and curled over his head, the sound of his bones popping. I think of Mom spinning me in the summer evenings to fly among the fireflies who blink and burn and disappear.

Sometimes, Jewel lets me stay all night, lets the sky silver and bruise before telling me her shift's over, and then I go and get in line and wait for work. Sometimes, the manager comes and says, will that be all for you tonight? And I pay and leave and walk until the sun comes up and think of the other half of my life that I have to pass into kiosk man's hands before I can exist outside Jewel's cartography.

In this way, inch by inch, dollar by dollar, I collect what I need to rediscover myself. Kiosk man had said five hundred and I give it to him. I give it to him because he is right: what is the cost of a life? What is the cost of knowing who you are?

In front of the vital statistics clerk, I use something imaginary to gain something real. And I am scared of being turned away, of being wrong where I was born, of the state having no record of me, of my ID being cut into pieces, of being arrested, but mostly of holding myself in my own hands.

I move the way I have always moved, along the roads, the painted lines of the asphalt, my river. I sleep where I have always slept: in the fields and parking lots, the blanket of the sky pulled down over me. I move south, because even in Richmond it's too cold to sleep at night.

And because I do not exist, I stand in parking lots in the purple dark of the morning. In the cold, the smoke of my breath burns through the spaces between my fingers, my red face next to the ash of the ones standing next to me. I have to stand apart, because to them I do not exist either.

On a day I am picked, I climb into the back of a pickup and am driven to a worksite and given a shovel and told to dig here or here, this hole or that trench, and my curved back becomes an iron piston that drives a space into the frozen ground. At night I rub petroleum jelly into the cracks of my skin and they burn.

And because I don't exist, I last seven days in my first parking lot before the others, who have refused to see me, realize I am there, realize they do not want me there with them, and they turn their fists on me. And because I am made of iron, I cannot feel them, so I make myself small and impenetrable, a turtle shell, and let their anger and fear and pain pour down the shell of my body.

It's okay, I say from the ground.

And they stop.

It's okay, I say. And I stand and pick up my backpack and shake their hands and walk away.

I move south and south and end up where I started. And because I don't exist, I carry a basket over my back and bend down to the strawberry bush and ask for its red fruit. Sometimes, the strawberry bush says yes, and sometimes it asks that I pay in blood. And because I don't exist, it doesn't matter that I find this feeling beautiful. And with my hands, I pinch the fruit and twist and put them in my basket, and when I put my basket onto the scales it is only my effort they are measuring, my value is measured in its weight.

Sometimes in the early evening, as the sun moves down below the palms, I put my basket down and stretch into the ache of my back, and when I breathe, I breathe in the fragrance of the strawberries I have crushed with my hands and rubbed into my skin. And I breathe into the resistance of my body to be straightened and feel as bright as the rose light blooming into the clouds in the sky.

But the winter strawberry season, too, does not last, so I move north again when the sun starts to burn rivulets of red on my arms and neck. And because I don't exist, I can move into a town at night and be in the parking lot the next morning waiting and sipping coffee with the others as if I had always been there and been picked to paint, or to dig, or clear debris. And sometimes I wonder if this is what Llewellyn meant when he said I was free to be as big as I wanted inside of a universe so small. But what we are doing doesn't feel like freedom.

My earliest memory is of a bonfire. I can feel the heat from it now pulling at the skin on my face, the blue at the center. In this memory, I still thought the blue was a ball of cold compressed down by all the heat around it. I know now that the blue at our center is heat compressed into heat.

Our bonfires run together, orange glowing ash twining and rising up from our bodies. I feel them in my body. I carry them everywhere I go. They are the waypoints of my memories. They stretch back and back, ash-rubbed and stained beneath my skin, memories before memories.

In my first memory, I remember there was a chill wind before the first match was struck. It must have been late in the summer or early autumn, us moving south to chase the warmth. I remember Mom's arms wrapped around me, warm skin against my cheek. We sat on a bale of hay and watched Llewellyn construct the pyramid, touch a match to the shaved bark at its center, blow soft and soft until the white smoke curled up through the logs and bloomed into fire.

Dad was there, too. And this is what I remember: him touching a harmonica to his lips and music like the echoes of a train cutting its horn through the fog at night. And I remember Llewellyn sitting down next to Dad and picking up his guitar and adding his music to Dad's, the music changing again like water dropping into a bucket, the bucket filling and filling and overflowing. And I remember the warmth of Mom's skin and the chill that ran beneath my own, moved down inside and danced, and how the music changed again like a bloom of color radiating from the fire, round and warm. And I remember being pulled up into the air, pulled up and up into Mom's arms and spun and danced, my body so cradled and safe. And how Mom sang. And I could feel her singing vibrating into me, her voice resonating through her chest into my ear. And how I closed my eyes and let the world spin. The sound of Dad's vibrating harmonica, Llewellyn's picking, sticks popping in the fire, Mom's voice deep inside her chest. Deep and deep.

And I thought, this is how I was made. I thought, this is where I came from—dance and smoke and a steel harmonica. And this feels true. This feels like where I began, where we began—Mom and Dad and me—the invention of our galaxy.

I've held on to this memory as long as I can, but I can't hear their voices anymore, can only see the shapes of them; and I can't reach out and touch my Mom's cheek, only feel the warmth of her skin against mine when the memory sparks in my dreams. My memories are made of static; they sting and pop and then dissipate if I try to touch them. And I wonder, now, where the memory goes when it pops, where that life went, wonder if it ever existed or if I shaped it from the fragments of other lives.

I am in a Waffle House in Staunton when this memory

blooms again. I am close to Harrisonburg. I am sitting at the counter. I have a mug of coffee in my hands. I reach down and take the envelope Rolfe gave me from my backpack. It is bigger than I remembered. I hold the heft of it in my hand. It feels heavy and deadly and beautiful there. I turn it over and pinch the clasp, keeping the flap closed, and look inside. There are ten envelopes inside, all wrapped in a rubber band. They are all addressed to me, sent to Rolfe's PO Box in Ocala. I wonder how many letters she sent to Dad before she gave up.

I flip through the postmarks, see them move from Harrisonburg north and north and then west. The last one is postmarked Sandusky, Ohio. I've never been to Ohio. If I close my eyes, I can't imagine its smell.

Mom's not where I thought, I tell my waitress.

How's that? she says.

She's right here, I say.

You're a strange cookie, aren't you?

Can I take that booth over there? And can I get a refill? I say.

Of course, she says.

I move into the booth, spread her letters out on the tabletop and open the first one.

I can't hear what Mom sang to me that night or see her face anymore.

My Dearest Son Daniel, I will send for you as soon as I get settled in. It is harder out here than I realized, but also more beautiful too. I have a job at a college (a real-life college), and I can't wait for you to see it and all the colorful students who got here with their little hats and their summer dresses and their sandals and their backpacks. I want to get you a backpack, too, one that you'll wear to school every day, and a new pair of shoes, and a Macintosh computer you can do your homework on in your bedroom (on your very own desk with your very own chair and your very own bed). As soon as I save enough to get a place big enough, I'll send for you.

My Son Daniel, I found a park you will just love with a silly slide that curls around a merry-go-round. I go there every day to watch the boys run and grab the merry-go-round's arms and pull and pull and pull with their hands and spin the other children until they can barely hold on anymore, and I can see your smiling face in the middle of that circle with all those other children laughing and getting dizzy and hugging each other. We will go there every day after school, and you can pick an ice cream cone and we will walk home and I will make you roasted chicken on a stick every night if you want, just as soon as I find a place big enough so you can have your own room. It's harder out here than I thought it would be, but it's also more beautiful too.

Dear Daniel, I'm writing to let you know that I had to move. My new address is on the envelope. I will send for you as soon as I find a new job.

Dear Daniel, I'm writing to let you know that I have to move. I promise. I had to move.

Son, it's harder out here then I thought, but I wanted to let you know I found a wonderful new job at an amusement park right on a lake. The lake is so big it looks like the ocean. There's even a beach. As soon as I save enough money, I'm going to send for you, I promise.

Daniel, I can't wait for you to see how big the roller coasters are here, and how much wood and steel they used to make them. It looks like a whole city lives under the rails. And how many lights they use to light them up at night and so many different colors too. I can see you now wanting to climb up into their scaffolding and live there.

Dear Danny, sometimes I think about the first time we let you go on to the Ferris wheel by yourself and how Joe Joe hung you up there for what seemed like hours, and I wanted to climb the arms of the Ferris wheel myself and sit beside you and ask what you were thinking about up there. You were so still and nothing but shadow. I could see your dad in you in that moment, so much of your dad and how still your dad gets when he's thinking about something, but how that stillness sometimes became something else. It was so hard. I was so proud and so scared seeing you up there all by yourself, your shadow so still. And I wanted to climb the arms of the Ferris wheel and sit next to you and hold you up there in the sky. Remember when we used to do that? I wanted to, but your dad said you were fine. You were in your own world and that was fine. But you were so little up there and your little arms holding the bar and your back so straight against the wind.

He's so proper, I said to your dad. And your dad just stood still and stared into the trees. And I wanted to just float up there, not even to touch you but to be close, just to float nearby and see what shape your eyes were and what you were looking at with your little back so straight against the wind and what that meant. It's harder than I ever thought to remember, but also more beautiful too.

Dear Daniel, I promise I'll send for you soon. I just want to find a place you'll be proud of, that you'll want to stay forever. It's hard out here. I want so much. I promise.

Son, you tell your dad to read you these letters if you don't know all the words yet.

Cedar Point is far bigger than I'd imagined when I imagined finding my mother here. Outside, more people are waiting to get in than have ever been to our carnival. The wood and steel scaffolds of its architecture reach up and up and out to what seems like an impossible distance. I wonder how many people are inside, how much space between each I'll have to move so I can find her, or would I be crushed by their collective mass, lost in their undulating colors? I walk and walk and walk and feel how big the universe has expanded for my mother, worry that I will not be able to find her within a circle so large. I hold her letters in my hands—the envelope Rolfe gave me. This is where they end. She is here or she is not here. What does it mean to be at the end of things?

I crouch down, smell the rubber burn of hot tar, let the bodies of those entering push past my balled self, sway me forward and back with their momentum. I am here. And in this crush of bodies, of legs moving and moving, the slap of feet against the asphalt, I can feel the bigness and smallness of what it means to look for her, to find her and to not find her. I hold the envelope in my hands and press her words into me. I look up into the faces of those pushing past me, see all of their excitement and joy tensed across their faces, the children holding the disembodied hands of their mothers and fathers, their faces turned to me as they walk past, and I crouch here and look and hold her letters in my hands so I can be looking and not looking, so that I can not be at the end of things just yet, so that maybe one of the bodies pushing past me at any particular moment would be my mother's even though I also know that if she were here, this is not the direction she would go.

I stay rooted here until the calves of my legs burn, until the sun moves from one side of the sky to the other, until the flow of legs around me reverses and the feet that danced toward the gates drag back and the lights of the park that once illuminated their stretched faces and left their smiles frozen move into shadow. I stay until the gates close and the ticket booths empty and the fireworks burst over the scaffold of the rides and the last of the riders stumble into the parking lot and the security guards loom over me and tell me it is time to go home.

I am home, I say.

Funny boy, they say.

And they push me down and drag me up and put me on a bus and say good night, pretty boy.

I come back and I come back. On the second day, they kick me in the head before dragging me to the bus. On the third day, they grab me by the hair and pull me up and tell me they are tired of seeing my face. On the fourth day, I am hungry so I load sacks of concrete for a contractor for fifty dollars and eat a lumberjack breakfast for dinner and three cups of coffee and stare into the blackness of my cup and there is the blue of Dad's eye opening in the dark, and there is the space where mother used to be. The waitress comes and asks if I want a fourth and I tell her there is no more room inside for any of it and then I drop the fifty dollars on the table and leave.

On the fifth day, sore and bruised, I am crouched next to a bed of flowers. The security guards bring their supervisor.

Why do you keep coming back? she says.

I am waiting for my mother.

Do you think she lives here or something?

If I stay out here, I don't have to choose, I say.

What the hell does that mean?

I hand the supervisor the letter, the last one I have. I say, if I choose to go in to find her, I might not find her. This way is safer. This way I don't have to do the choosing.

The supervisor looks at the letter and reads it and stays silent for a long time, says, Jesus Christ. Says, come with me. Says, employees don't leave from these gates.

And I get up and follow the supervisor and my legs burn from the crouching and the lifting of the concrete and I have to drag them across the pavement to follow her and each step feels like I am pulling the roots of my legs from deep in the ground. The supervisor talks into her radio and stops by a different gate and tells me to wait. And I wait. And the rides, which held stars in the scaffolds of their bodies, blink off.

I stand alone under the lights of a walkway. I see my mother limping out of the gate with the supervisor, the curls of her hair spilling from under a visor. I feel the boundaries of my body disappear and there is no ground or sky or weight or weightlessness or body or gravity or light or dark, and I cannot tell where my body ends and the light I am standing under begins, and my mother holds my face in her hands and looks into my eyes and I fold myself until I am small enough to fit into the space between those hands and she whispers, oh my sweet, sweet boy. And every part of me crashes into those words.

How? she says. How?

It doesn't matter, I say. Because everything that led to this moment only matters to me.

How? she asks again.

Rolfe, I say.

And she nods and grabs my hand and holds it to her chest and we stand in silence because Rolfe is enough.

Mother says, I have a den you can sleep in. It has a couch and a blanket and a fan for you. She says, I promise to get a mattress as soon as I can. I like to sleep with a fan, she says. It reminds me of the road. You might like to sleep with one too. She says, I don't have much to eat right now, but I promise tomorrow I will go and buy us a nice chicken and some potatoes and roast veggies and we can sit around the kitchen table and have a proper dinner. She says, there is cheese and crackers if you want. She says, I have a TV. Sometimes when I have trouble sleeping it helps me, so it might help you too. She says, I picked up extra shifts this week, but I promise on my first day off we will do something special. She says, I have a jar of peanut butter. You can make yourself a sandwich if you get hungry while I am at work. She says, I only get three channels clearly, but it keeps me company. It might keep you company while I'm at work, so you can leave it on if you get lonely. She says, if you want a job, I can talk to my boss for you. She says, wouldn't it be fun to work together again?

These are my friends from work, she says. I've told them all about you. And her friends circle and preen and touch my hair, always my hair, and tell me how my hair is just like my mother's, only darker. And they say how tall I am, and beautiful too, and how I must be a lady killer, and how little Daniel isn't so little anymore. So dangerous with those eyes, they say. We could just melt. And then they disappear, and so does mother, and I am left in a room full of the photographs of my past selves staring back at me. Who were you? I ask to the pictures of myself. Then I turn off the television and walk out the door.

Some days I bring a cup of coffee and go to the lake and stare from the shore at the great towers of metal and wood and feel the vibration of their carriages spinning circles in the sky, and the faces of the riders, grown large as moons, hang in the distance like a time lapse needlepoint filling the spaces in between. And there is Mother with her friends telling stories of little Daniel and how he clung to his mother in the dark on the Ferris wheel, because even from here the Ferris wheel is at the center. Some days I go to the arcade and I put quarters into Galaga and Time Warriors and Double Dragon so that I don't have to be myself, so that a life that is not me could exist for as long as I had quarters to renew it. And some days I look for work, anything that would occupy and punish my body, so that I could feel something else besides a dull throb behind my eyes, a sickness creeping into my joints, because this is what it feels like to be adrift. And when I am done, I turn and go back to Mother's apartment, make a peanut butter sandwich, turn on the television and sleep and sleep and sleep.

And my mother returns and she returns and she returns. And she says, such a long day on my feet. And she says, how was your day? And she says, there is cheese and crackers if you get hungry. And she lays her head back in her chair and stares at the television, and the drone of the voices comes through the screen. And she says, I have a day off coming soon. We could do something special. And then her eyes close and she is gone and I am alone again.

On the twelfth day she opens the door and I stand up and Mother limps over, cradles my face. You've been sleeping all day, she says.

I was tired.

It's good to sleep sometimes. And she sits in her chair, lifts her foot, says, can you help me? She says, I've been on my feet all day. It is not so easy anymore.

Ten years, Mom, I say. Ten years.

Please, she says. I'm so tired.

Okay, I say. And I take her shoe in my hand, untie it, pull and pull and then I hold her foot, red and swollen and sweaty and hot in my hands, and Mother lets out a sigh and she says, it's so hard. And she says, there's cheese and crackers if you get hungry. And she leans back in her chair and closes her eyes and her mouth hangs open and her breath fills the room. Ten years, I say.

I let go of her swollen foot and let it fall to the floor and look around her room at the television's quiet glow, the crusted plates on the coffee table, the picture of me with no front teeth smiling from the back of one of Llewellyn's ponies, her slack and breathing face, and inside the darkness of her mouth I wish there is a safety I can crawl into.

I buy a ticket at the box office and pour through the turnstiles with the others. I walk the concourse, the gift shops, gamer's alley, and listen to the cadence of their pitch. I buy a funnel cake and hold the warmth of the paper plate in my hands and eat in the shade of a roller coaster whose steel body resonates like a song when the train rolls over me. I dream myself among its beams as if I can make my home in its timbers, feel the rumble of its body in my sleep. I go to the sea of my mother's letters, sit on its shore with a lemonade and stare into the deep. I find the tallest roller coaster I can, sit in the front, feel the weight of the world pulling me down as the train pulls me up and up and up, my back pressed into the seat, the sky pulled closer and then I hang over the earth, staring down into the concrete and steel and color of the people down below, their eyes watching the train inch its way over the crest, the front of the train being pulled slow and slow over the edge and then the drop and the speed and the wind cooling the sweat from my body and I am pulled upward again and to the left and I feel the weight of all that gravity pushing me down into my seat and we crest another hill, fast and fast this time, and I feel the coaster try to fling my body out into the universe, out and up, and I am weightless and my body feels free and loose and expansive, and then I am slammed down into my seat again and to the right, the pull of gravity, all that weight and I feel heavy and small and rooted and beautiful inside my seat and then we are flung into the dark and there are pinpoints of light that float in front of my eyes, and then we are spit out back into the bright and the wind and the warmth and the cheers of my fellow travelers and I step off and my feet feel as though nothing is solid anymore and I wobble and I expand and expand until my eyes are as big as Ferris wheels and I pop and liquefy.

My feet ache from the concrete, from this permanent carnival, but I walk and walk and the sweat pools in my lower back and everyone blurs together and I am lost, but in the moment when the sky burns itself out and the lights of the rides burn themselves on, I pause and hold my breath like everyone else. And in that pause, I see my mother holding single roses wrapped in plastic walking among the crowd, pausing to talk, holding out her rose offerings, reaching into her fanny pack for change. I see her and I see myself passing change through the open window, feel the cool night air on my forearms as they take the funnel cake from my hands.

I see my mother and see her small and alone and caught within the incandescent lights of the midway and realize she hasn't been able to escape what it was she was trying to escape. She has only replaced transience with intransigence, the traveling carnival for the permanent one, one fantasy with another. I wonder if I stay how far, really, am I moving away from the circle Dad created for me. And I wonder how far any of us can stray from the orbit of the universe our parents create for us. And if I stay, will I fall into the event horizon of my mother's fantasies?

I turn to a boy, maybe eleven, and I pass a twenty into his hands. And I tell him to buy a rose from that woman over there, the one with the curly gray-gold hair, and to give it to that girl, the one with the unicorn hat on. And I press an envelope into his hand, the one Rolfe gave me so long ago, and I tell him to pass this to the woman when he buys the rose from her. And I tell him I don't care about the change.

I watch him go, uncertain and wobbly, through the crowd. I see him ask for a rose. My mother gives it to him. I see him pause and look down. I see my mother turn away from him and begin to walk away. I see the boy hold the envelope at his side and watch her back as she leaves. I lose my mother in the crowd, her hair lost in the sea of bodies around her. She reappears. The boy has the envelope held out in front of him. He looks down at it. He looks back at me. My mother hands a rose out for a mother who bends down and gives it to her daughter. I nod at the boy. Go, I say with my eyes. Go. He runs to my mother, taps her shoulder, hands her the envelope and runs away. I see her look down at it, see her recognize what is contained inside. And in this moment, I turn away and leave and when my mother looks up and searches the crowd for the face of her son, she will search for the eight-year-old boy she left behind instead of the eighteen-year-old who is walking away from her.

I learned to read curled up with Mom on the floor of our van, the wind blowing the trailer back and forth across the highway behind us in the dark, the feel of the rumble strips as Dad fell asleep in the front. The jerk of his head, the roll of the van back into the center of the lane. She held a flashlight in one hand and the flashcards in the other. On days off, she would take me to the library, and I would sit in her lap and she would read to me. In Woodbridge, there was a library that had a reading room made of stairs and thick carpet and tunnels to crawl through, and she would follow me around with a book in her hand and read to me. And I would crawl through the tubes and listen to her voice, muted and soft, reciting to me the cadence of the language in the books she held in her hand. Whisk achoo, said the wolf in the darkness outside of the children's bedroom.

In Ellicott City, the library had a card catalog as big as a house, and Mom would riffle through the pages while I walked through the aisles, arms outstretched, touching the books on either side with my fingertips, listening to the rumble of spine on spine. Whisk achoo, said the librarian from her desk.

In Clearwater, Mom would take books from a basket

under her bed and we would float in the water and she would sing the words into the sky, and I would lie back into the water, float inside of her language, and stare up into the blue and imagine the worlds she created on its canvas.

Dad taught me to count, said I needed to know how to make change in my head if he was going to trust me at the window. Stripping down after dark, he'd say something like $5.95, they give you a twenty. I was supposed to count back the imaginary change the way he wanted me to—a nickel is six, seven, eight, nine, ten, and ten will give you twenty. What's the tax on ten bucks? He'd ask scraping the fryers into our fat bucket. What state? I was supposed to ask. Virginia. Five cents, rounded, I'd say. He'd nod his head and tell me to sweep out the floors or wash down the sifter or wipe down the sign. In this way, I learned to add, subtract, do fractions.

After Sandusky, I decide to stay in one place. I take a bus to Columbus, and because I now exist, I find a job loading trucks at a warehouse. On days I don't work, I go into the public library and pull books at random from the return cart and read. Sometimes I go and pull a stick from the periodicals section and read the newspaper, but it is hard to concentrate on what is happening, because what is happening to me exists only in the pull of my muscles in my back, in the time I punch in and the time I punch out, in the moments I am able to sit and pull off my boots and exhale. I only care about what was possible inside of words, and so I go to the library and I look through what others have found beautiful and pull from their lists and read until the library is closed.

One day I walk in and see on the desk a sign that says, *Earn your GED and start the life you want.*

I say to the man behind the counter, what's this?

He says, what? And he looks at what I was pointing at. The GED?

Yes.

He looks at me for a long time and then says, it's like a high school diploma.

And I don't have to go to school for it?

Nope. You only have to be over eighteen and take a test.

And so I start coming to the library on my days off to learn biology and history and algebra, too. And for the first time, when I look in the places where my mother and father lived inside of my imagination, I see a blank in the spaces where my mother and father used to be, and I start to fill those spaces with other worlds, worlds real and not real, the ones I find in the books pulled from the shelves, and those worlds merge with my memories, and in my dreams instead of myself I become those others I read about, and instead of my life, I live in the worlds those words create for me.

And I realize this is what it means to move in my own orbit, to see nothing but space around me and to move inside of it wherever I want to go. And I fill that space with whatever I want, test how far I can run away from my origin, to see if I can reach terminal velocity and leave the universe I have always known, the one my mother could never really break away from. And I read and I imagine and I push and push and push on the boundaries, but I can't tell if I am breaking free of the gravity that holds me or if I'm just spinning in place.

We move in circles, Llewellyn used to tell me, radiate out from the center and move in our own orbits, the center of gravity always pulling us back to the middle. In order to stay, my movements had to become smaller, the circles I moved in for work had to become blocks instead of cities, states. I load trucks on some days before the sun comes up, on others I spray the dust down on construction sites, on weekends I am a barback downtown where I refill ice wells, switch kegs, bring clean glasses from the dishwashers in the kitchen.

I do not matter outside of the services my body can provide, so I am free to drift in and out of these roles so long as my back still bends, my arms lift what needs to be lifted, my feet carry a weight to where it needs to be carried; my mind can move in any direction it wants so long as it also holds the next task after the one my body is currently performing.

When I go back into the kitchen I am invisible so long as I stay away from the orbits of the cooks. And because I do not exist, I am free to watch and to see and to learn how each person behind the counter is linked together, how they matter, how connected they are, how they move inside of their own universe, but also how those universes orbited each other, touch and pass their energies from one to the next to the next in a chain, how that energy builds something beautiful, how that chain is impenetrable to any force from the outside; how little my utility matters outside of the immediate need for ice, for water, for a clean glass.

Llewellyn said focus on what is right in front of me, and what is in front of me is a circle whose bright heat and energy I want to enter, but I am floating somewhere in the darkness outside of it. So I apply and I apply and I apply until a restaurant called Papillon allows me to become a prep cook, and I learn how to hold a utility knife and how to use that utility in the ways I need it, how to pay attention, how to commit my movements to memory so that they stay locked there when I need them, and because I matter now it matters that I find this feeling beautiful.

And I wonder, how far away can one travel from their center? This kitchen looks nothing like the kitchen in the trailer, my father's double fryers, the prep table behind, the finishing table to the left; this kitchen, large and expansive and clean and gleaming, has room to move and room to be isolated in your task. But the dance is the same. Our station dictates our movement. We move in precise ways. And if we have to move from our station, we announce our movements so the dance does not falter, does not collapse in on itself.

Now, I wake in the pink of early morning every day and ride my bike to the restaurant so I can start dinner prep. When I first started, the others called me princess, called me beautiful, kissed the air when I walked in, asked if I had a pussy under my apron and lifted it to take a peek. Don't pay attention to those assholes, the sous-chef said. This is what they do before they let anyone into their circle. Just be glad you aren't an actual woman, like me. And so I shave the curls from my head and work with my sleeves rolled up to show the scars on my arms, and so the softness of my face and the hardness of my body confuses and silences them.

I learn to curl my fingers under my knife, learn the sound a fish makes when its skin crisps and is ready to be turned over, learn the color of sugar just before it burns so that it will run rich and sticky and sweet over the cake. I learn the softness of medium rare, the firmness of well-done, how to tell by pressing my fingertips into the flesh. I learn to distrust a customer who orders their steak medium-well. I learn the beauty of a plate and how a proper sear will make your under-cooked steak taste "perfect." I learn that color and texture and freshness means elevation, means precision, means extravagance. This is what they pay us for, the sous-chef tells me. She shows me how to swirl the Brussels sprouts with sauce—balsamic reduction, they call it—how to wipe the plate clean before setting it on the counter. First you learn to plate, then you learn to cook, the sous-chef says.

Respect the rules, she says, and you will be fine. And so I do not peek at the pastry chef as he kneads the dough, do not watch the saucier worry over his beurre blanc, do not study the prep cooks filleting the salmon so that their carcasses glow pink and translucent when they lift them into the trash can, do not question how long a bone marrow must boil in the pot so that its juices reveal a broth. I pay attention to the whiteness of my plate, the swirl of the black glaze over my asparagus, the shock of the purple pansy placed on top of the white slice of cake, the swirl of raspberry glaze around its base. In this way, I remember Dad's first lesson, his concentrated pours over the hot oil, the flicker of his wrist as he finished one funnel cake and started another, the precision of his arm as he mixed the dry ingredients, how he measured the water and tested the thickness of the batter, how he thumped the sifter of powdered sugar over the finished cake, still hot and steaming and taking the sugar into itself, how he passed it through the open window like an offering, like a host.

You have to respect the ingredients if you are going to cook, the sous-chef tells me one day. I am chopping vegetables before lunch service. She walks behind me. You must know the ingredients to respect them, she says. She draws a cloth napkin across my eyes and ties it, the warmth of her presses against me. She passes a fork into my hand. Taste this, she says. What is it?

Steak, I say.

Lamb, you idiot, she says. Pay attention. She smacks me in the forehead. Think, she says. She passes another fork, and this?

Salmon.

Snapper. Am I wasting my time here?

No.

Notice how the fat flavors the flesh. Notice the difference between lean and fatty, moist and dry. Notice the texture, how much your jaw has to work to release the juices. Pay attention. She hands me another fork.

Pork, I say.

What part?

I chew and chew. Belly, I say.

Tenderloin. But better, closer, she says. Pay attention.

This is venison, she says. And this is halibut and this is lobster and this is duck.

I taste and I taste. Without my eyes, I have to rely on my mouth, my jaw, my tongue to understand what is being passed to me, to roll it around and let it touch all the parts of my mouth, to feel the oily duck fat coating the flesh, to feel the resistance of the pork chop against my teeth, the give of the scallop on my tongue.

I learn the rules are rigid, textures and flavors you can and cannot mix, balance that must be established in certain ways; but inside those rules, I am free to move in as many directions as I want, and so I can make my station as big as I want so long as I move within the circle the rules have created for me. The alchemy of cooking has no end and no beginning.

Hey, hey, where did you go, space cadet, the sous-chef asks me.

Everything is illuminated, I tell her.

What the hell does that mean?

I'm just getting started, I said.

Just finish those vegetables before service, she says.

Learn the ingredients, the sous-chef told me, so in the summer I add Pearl Market to my own small orbit around the restaurant and the library. I ride my bike to Gay Street and park and walk from booth to booth and see the yellows and reds and greens, the purple from the eggplant, the smell of the rose mallows and lavender and black-eyed Susans. I ask the vendors about minerals and water and sun and rain. I taste the honey and with my tongue understand the difference between clover, wildflower, buckwheat, goldenrod. I get a sandwich and sit and watch the street musicians or the jugglers or the dancers and put a dollar in their hat or case and take my bags home and combine and taste and recombine in endlessly unappetizing ways.

I am walking out of Pearly Alley with a bundle of cherries and peas and summer squash one day when I see a tree walking down the street, its branches swinging low against the sidewalk. It stops and curls its fingers around the shoulders of a woman who hugs the trunk and smiles. A man takes their picture. The branches curl around a dollar and it disappears somewhere inside of its trunk and it bows low, its branches outstretched to the tree's side, and the leaves of its crown brush against the top of the woman's head. Then the tree ambles on, finds a boy walking with his mother, and the tree puts its branch around the boy's shoulder and the boy, nervous, scratches his knee and tries to smile and the mother takes the picture and they walk away and the tree bows its head, its crown rustling in the wind. And it turns and sees me with its great googly eyes, and it unzips itself and folds back its crown and Daniel, red-faced and smiling, says, I cannot believe it's you.

I say, how did you find me?

And he says, boy, you did a lot more than just run away inside of your head, didn't you?

And I say, why are you here?

And he says, the same as you, trying to experience the world.

That sounds like a bunch of bullshit.

Bullshit and fantasy are what I peddle in, he says. He takes a rag from around his neck, wipes his red face. I wasn't looking for you, he says. My partner is at the university taking a workshop, and I thought why not be a tree while I'm sitting around doing nothing.

We move in different orbits, but sometimes they touch.

Exactly. You remember that, huh? So, what are you doing here?

I tell him I'd left to find my mother, but when I found her I found there was a sadness to her fantasies that mirrored the violence of my father's, and so I could not stay. So now I am here and have discovered food in a different way. And that I love the dance of the kitchen, how we move to the metronome of the tickets, how we communicate our movements so no one moves in ways that are out of step with the beat that has been established. And so I am training to be a chef. And I work for Papillon and would love for him to come so I could plate his food.

And he says, maybe we will.

And he folds the crown back over his head and zips himself back into a tree. And he bows and I bow and he ambles away.

Two weeks later, I get a phone call while prepping for dinner service. The sous-chef yells, hey, two minutes and holds the phone out to me. I hold it to my ear and say, hello?

From the other side Rolfe says, your father.

What about him?

And Rolfe tells me after I left my father stopped talking to anyone, stopped coming by for a beer or conversation or song, stopped taking care of himself, and so when a cut on his leg would not heal and turned red then black then ballooned his calf and he couldn't walk anymore, they had to take him to the hospital and the doctors cut and cut and cut away at the infection until they eventually had to remove everything below his knee. And now he's in the hospital and no one can work his booth, and they can only hold it open for so long before they have to give it to someone else, and if he can't follow them to the next place, then they have to do what they have to do and there's nothing else that can be done.

All of this takes longer than two minutes to tell me. The sous-chef stares at me from her station. My chef's knife sits on the chopping block next to the tomatoes I was dicing. I want to pick up the chef's knife, chop a piece of myself off—my ear or my hand or my foot—instead, I put down the phone, pick up the knife, hold the blade against my forearm, feel the cold steel pressed there.

Let the knife do the work, the sous-chef always says.

I drag the blade across my skin.

This is how my circle is closed, how the center calls me home: I am standing in the door frame of Dad's room in the hospital. The blue universe of his eyes frame me inside of themselves and I am small again, small and standing next to him in the funnel cake booth, the light of the carnival pouring out into the black; sitting behind him in the truck being cradled by the evening rain as we move through the world, in perpetual circuit; squatting underneath the table in our trailer with him in the dark; bringing him back from places I could not see or know or understand. I am looking at him. He is looking at me. I do not move.

He gestures me over into the half-moon of his curtain. He does not smile, the muscles of his face unable to move in those directions anymore. I sit down on the place on the bed where his calf should have been and I see the part of Dad's leg above the knee move over to make room for me as if his leg, too, thinks it still occupies that space.

So you've become a man finally, he says.

Maybe, I say.

How did you find out?

I know everything. I've always known everything. This is what you have taught me. Remember—what the carnival taught me—to see everything?

He waves his hand. Don't bullshit me with that story bullshit.

The tree found me, I tell him. And then so did Rolfe.

Rolfe is good people.

So is Daniel.

He looks at me, unsure which Daniel I am talking about. So what have you been doing with yourself all these years?

Is this what you really want to talk about? I say.

He sighs. Shakes his head.

I didn't think so, I say.

He looks out the window, tells the window, the trees outside, I need you. And he says, they will replace me if you don't take over. And he says, you are the only one who knows.

I tell him that it has been years and it is not in me anymore.

And he tells me there is no such thing as not knowing anymore. And he tells me to remember the circle and to remember what belongs inside of it and he tells me to remember I stood beside him in the circle and because of that I know what he knows and I always will. Remember the eight, he says.

And I look at the frame of my father tucked in underneath the fleece blue hospital blanket, small and alone, and remember my father could not exist anywhere else and that being replaced meant being nonexistent, and so I am already standing inside of his trailer, already pouring the oil into his fryers, already opening the valves of the propane tanks, already rolling the awning open and turning on its yellow sign and pulling the mixture into shape with my hands and holding my wrists over the oil so I can flick the cakes into life.

And so I tell him he will not lose himself, that losing his leg will not result in the absence of the rest of him, that he can count on me to fold back into who I was for him until he could be made whole again, but that I cannot stay, cannot stay and take care of him beyond that.

And he says, thank you. And he says, thank you. And he says, thank you.

And I tell him nothing and walk out.

And here is the gray in Joe Joe's hair, the wrinkles around his smile. Here is the grip on my shoulder, heavy and tight and beautiful. And here is Rolfe, a slight limp now from his hip. And here is the Ferris wheel and Dad's funnel cake trailer. And Rolfe says, what does this mean? And I tell him, I don't know. And he nods and the lion pulls on its chain and welcomes me with a yawn.

I walk to the trailer, pull Dad's keys out and unlock the door and walk in. And here is my mother and here is my mother and here is my mother, the presence of her absence heavy and deadly. I close the circle tight so I can fit inside the smallest possible space I can, pull rubber gloves onto my hands, take the fryers out from their housings, and I plunge my hands down into hot soapy water and begin to scrub. And with my body, this is how I return.

When we can, we make a circle with our trailers and spiral outward, the arms of our tents and canopies reaching toward the boundaries of the fences we so often move into. And in this adopted place, after the incandescent lights of the carnival have burned and faded and gone dark, after the Ferris wheel has finished its last rotation around the sky, we bring what we can to the center we have made, build a fire, and burn everything we have held in during the day, let it get pulled out of us, dry and crisp and flake away. It is at this bonfire the day after I return that I tell Rolfe and Joe Joe that before I left the restaurant the owner had pulled me aside and said he wanted to send me to New York where I could get proper training, said he's got a restaurant there where I could work while I went to school and he would pay for my tuition. He said, listen, this is how good I think you can be. He said, I get this thing with your dad. I do. But the best I can do is give you three weeks to work it out. But if you don't come back or don't call me and tell me you are flying to New York, then don't bother. I'll move on and you'll move on and that's it. This is a big bet on you. Don't let me down.

Easy choice, Joe Joe says.

How easy is it? Here is Rolfe handing me a beer from the cooler. Here is Joe Joe making a joke about a woman, her body, and his hook. Here is the warmth of the fire and the warmth of the hay bale I am sitting on. Here is the dark of the sky above my head and the dry grass beneath my feet. Here is the black scaffolding of the rides standing in the darkness around me. Here is Llewellyn's stare out over the field, out into the stand of trees, his marble eyes burning. All of these things are my mothers and fathers and brothers and sisters, my home and my yard and my shelter and my world. How easy is it to make the decision to leave a second time?

I stand and walk over to Llewellyn. I am almost as tall as he is now. The skin on his face has crisped, turned to parchment. What now? I ask him. I look out over the field with him, tip my beer to his lips to wet them so he can speak, but all of his words have dried up. I put my arm around his shoulder, feel the hollow cage of his body tip into me. I put the beer to my own lips. My tongue is dry. The beer washes over it like sandpaper.

Behind me, a wrestling match starts. I hear the wet smack of bodies, the taunts thrown into the middle, arms reaching for advantage, hands parrying them away. Shirts are removed. Their backs glisten in the glow of the fire. One of them is thrown over the other's hip, falls into the dirt and grass and mud. A hoot escapes my lips. He rolls in the dust, rolls to his feet, lunges at the other's hips and drags him down. They are both now covered in dirt and grass and hay. The man on the bottom pushes the chin of the man on the top of him up and back, seems to fold his body in half and wraps his legs around the other's neck and pulls. He has him now in an arm lock. There is a tap, tap, tap on the ground and Rolfe stands and declares the winner, gives him a beer. I tip mine to the loser, give him a turn at the bottle. Another man, someone I don't know, walks in with a guitar, sits down and begins to pluck at the strings, pulls blue grass up through his body and out into the air. His feet stamp a beat in the dust. A woman I don't know begins to sing. Her voice rises and falls like a tide over the rhythm. Joe Joe stands and starts a dance, holds his hook over his head. His hook glimmers in the light of the fire. He twirls and twirls and stamps his feet. Get your ass out here, he says to me. I join him, stamping the beat into the ground, stamping it deep down into the earth so that the core of the earth can also resonate to the rhythm of the song. I crouch down, fold myself into the harmony. And here is Dad being fitted with his new leg, being helped to his feet, taking his first halting steps; and here is Mom sitting in front of the television, alone, her feet in a salt bath, eating soup from a bowl. A girl about four-years-old holds her arms up for her mother to lift her. Her mother pulls her up into her arms and dances her around the fire in little circles. A fiddle joins the guitar, playing over the top of his harmony. The guitarist pushes the rhythm forward, his fingers disappear into the strings, the notes chase each other. My feet struggle to keep up. Those who watch start to clap on the offbeat. The woman singing calls and the rest respond with shouts, with hoots; they jump up and down as the guitar picks faster and faster. The fiddle saws to keep up. I spray my beer into the air, foam burned orange in the fire. I lock elbows with Joe Joe and we spin. Three children come from the shadows carrying small bundles of dry leaves and twigs close to their chests, an offering. They walk to the bonfire and toss their bundles in and the bonfire cracks and pulses and pushes their offering up into the night sky.

What is New York to me in this moment? Nebulous, ephemeral, uncertain: a possibility. Here, in this darkness, these images, these people, the heat of this fire, the sound of the wind in the trees around us, the open field, the lumbering hulk of the rides standing watch, all of this feels easy; the gravity of this place pulls so strong, pulls me into its memory, back into its body. It is so easy to remember this, the laughter behind me, the liquid flow of these friendships, to forget what is outside of it, the life I have carved for myself outside of this orbit, this circle.

Your dad existed here because he couldn't exist anywhere else, I think I hear Llewellyn tell me. But when I turn to listen, to hear him, his dead eyes stare out into nothing.

We are not here for your amusement, for your entertainment; these are not games to us. We are here to take your money and in exchange provide for you an illusion of competence, a fantasy of heroism and accomplishment. We are the sellers of your dreams. We will take your money so that in your winning you may feel superior to our games, superior to us, superior to the you that stood here before the winning. And so the words we sing, the siren song of our cadence, is the epic tale of your winning, the promise of glory on our battlefield.

Hey, be a winner, be a winner. You want to be a winner, right? We have nothing but winners here.

Winners all day.

Easiest games here.

All you need to win is to have an arm. You have an arm, right?

Look how simple this game is. Look how easy. Look how easy. This isn't hard, folks.

Let me show you how this works.

If I can do it, anyone can do it.

We have the most winners, we have the best winners, winners all day long.

You want to be a winner, right?

You, right there in the sweater, you look like a winner. Step on up here and win for your girl.

That's not your girl? Win for her anyway. You can make her your girl. All you have to do is win.

Win a bear for your mother, for your sister, for your daughter, for your wife. We have the best bears, the biggest bears, bears so big you'll need a truck bed to haul them around.

Win a bear for yourself.

You look like you have a big arm. Test your strength, test your strength, test your strength. Ring the bell and win, win, win, win, win.

Look at those arms. Is that sweater going to be able to contain those arms?

Three tries for five. Ring the bell three times and you can take home my wife.

Let me guess your weight. Let me guess your age. Let me guess your sign. I won't even make you take off that sweater.

Just need one more to play.

There we are, folks, there we are. Step on up.

Don't be shy, ladies. Show up your man. Win a bear for your man. He's not your man? Do you want him to be? Win a bear.

All you have to do is hit that target, hit the target right three times and you can be a hero. That's all you have to do.

Just need one more to play.

Let me see. Can you hide yourself? All you have to do to win is fool me.

Come on, folks, come on, just one more, one more, one more and we can get started.

Hey, hey, we have the first winner of the day!

Sean starts coming "just for a taste" in the early morning while I test the batter. He comes and knocks and places an orb of fried dough in his mouth and chews. And when he closes his eyes and tips his head back and hums, I know the batter is ready.

What do you do that makes your funnel cakes so much better? he asks.

I tell him I cast magic spells, that the secret is in the pour, that when you move your wrist in certain ways, it pours the magic from your hand. I tell him the yeast I use is ancient and has been cultivated for centuries and has been passed from my ancestors, from father to son, and cannot be found anywhere else on the planet, even though I use no yeast in the batter.

This is how he enters my orbit, with his rat tail braided down his back and his bare-footed run through the midway and his side-eyed smile and his little fists thrust in the air when I pass him his first tester of the day through the window of my trailer.

There is an attention, I say, that is absent in most. And that's what you need to do. Pay attention. Focus on what is right in front of you. When you stop paying attention, everything that matters goes away.

Okay, he says, shoving in mouthfuls and mouthfuls of fried dough.

Pay attention, I say.

And he stops and he swallows, then takes one more and holds the piece in his mouth and closes his eyes and lets the sugar melt around the dough and chews slowly, slowly, and opens one eye real small and slow and says, like that?

Stop being an idiot, I say.

He smiles and runs off with his rat tail braided and bobbing behind him and his bare feet cutting a path through the dust. This is our ritual.

One day I am coming through the parking lot with two sacks of flour over each shoulder and see him with his father off to the side, his father with a fist full of braid ripping Sean's head back so he can look at him. I see his father raise his hand and smack him across the face and then rip him upright when he tries to sink down into the mud, into the dirt, disappear below the cars and grass. And I see his father close a fist, and I yell, hey!

And I yell, hey!

I walk over with the two sacks slung over my shoulder. His father says, what the fuck do you want?

And I say, your anger is useless. And I say, movement is an illusion. And I say, every moment is beautiful, so pay attention, because when you stop paying attention and try to compare it to your expectations and make your judgments and become angry, everything becomes dark and you can't see anymore.

And his father looks at me, looks at the two fifty-pound

sacks of flour slung over my shoulder and lets him go and says, you're a strange cookie, aren't you?

And I say to Sean, I could really use your help with this sack of flour here.

And the father pushes Sean on the back of the head, tells him to sack up and stop crying and help this man with his flour.

Taking the fryers out one night after the lights of the carnival are extinguished and only the lights of our trailers illuminate the spaces between, I see him crouched in the dust under the orange arc lamps of a barn with a man in his fifties or sixties looming over him, whose back is set in a permanent crouch, whose knee wobbles and buckles as he stands. The man's mouth moves and Sean looks into the dust and makes himself smaller, and with each shrink into himself the man takes another step and another, his mouth moving, Sean shrinking into himself, the man moving. I walk over with my cutting knife in my hand and say, hey. I say, I could really use your help with the fryers. The man looks at my hands and says, we are just having a conversation. He's such a lovely young man—so smart, so many ideas. His single tooth moves in his mouth like a hatchet cutting his words. And I say, of course he is. He's my boy. He better be. And I say, how about those fryers? And the man says, you have such a lovely son there, sir. And I say, fuck off. And Sean looks at me confused. And I say, come on.

Another day, I watch his braid flying through the air be- hind him as he runs in front of my trailer, three boys chasing after him, one boy reaching out and grabbing the rat tail and dragging Sean to the ground and the others swarming with their teeth bared and their wild howls and their tiny fists and feet sinking into him. His little body curls into itself and his hands cover his face, and those fists and those feet on his spine and his kidneys and his head and the parts of his face that are not protected. I walk out with my tongs still dripping hot oil and I press the tongs into the arm of one of the boys and he yells and jumps back and the others run.

And I crouch down into the dust next to him, take a folding knife from my pocket, grab his rat tail in my hand and saw it off. I give it to him and say, you've got to make yourself as small as possible. And tears fall off his chin into the dirt. And I say, draw a circle in the ground around you. And I take my finger and draw a circle in the dirt, and he looks at me, then down at the ground, then takes his finger and does the same. And I say, now throw that rat tail as far as you can. And I say, everything that belongs to you is in the circle. And he chokes and he heaves and tears puddle on his cheeks and he says, but there's nothing in the circle. And I say, everything is inside the circle. And I say, and you have to protect it, because no one else will. And I say, now come on, let's get you cleaned up.

This is how I enter his orbit.

The lion becomes tired and arthritic and moody. Rolfe can no longer contain him with his eyes or hands or careful movements. The lion strains against the chain and howls and roars, and the sounds he makes fill the whole world with pain, fill our bodies with a resonate ache that vibrates more in our bones than in our ears. And the people come to see the lion, to see the lion rip Rolfe apart, to see the fangs sink deep into the neck flesh of Rolfe—Rolfe a limp child in his jaws—instead of to take pictures with him.

And so Rolfe goes to the lion when everyone is asleep, goes to the lion and takes off his clothes and leans against him naked and whispers to him it will be okay. And the lion breathes and breathes against him and moans. And Rolfe folds himself into the lion's mane until his skin becomes the lion's skin, until his heat becomes the lion's heat. And he takes a syringe and presses it into the lion's neck, plunges the liquid in. And the lion breathes and breathes and Rolfe rises and falls, rises and falls. And he tells the lion that he was a good lion, that he was beautiful. And the lion breathes and closes his eyes and goes to sleep. And Rolfe rises and falls and rises and falls, then rests and presses his face into the lion's neck and folds the lion's paw over his body and sleeps.

Later, Rolfe hangs the lion's body from a tree and drains his blood down into a pit he digs beneath him. And when it is done, when the lion is drained and hollow, he covers the pit with dirt and brings the lion down and unzips his skin and burns the lion's old body, the old broken and arthritic body, in the bonfire, takes the ashes and wears them around his neck in a pouch.

And he builds the lion a new body made of wire and wood and bone. And he takes the lion's skin and rubs salt in layer by layer with his hands and lets it dry for days and days until it becomes immortal. And he takes the new body and stuffs it with a new musculature made of soft things that do not fail or rot so easily, takes the lion's skin, dried and cured and beautiful, and stitches the lion back together, gives him new eyes made of amber—the color of wheat. And he gives the lion a new posture, one crouched and dangerous, the eyes peering into us, staring in like they always have, alive and deadly and beautiful.

He does all of this behind a tent he makes from great strips of primary-colored sails he hangs from a tree. And when he is done, he pulls down the sails and shows us the lion and we tell him he is beautiful and we tell him we are sorry. He says, I bought the lion as a cub from an exotic pet guy over the phone and it came in a crate in the back of a truck. I had always meant to stuff the lion, that the lion's purpose was always to be stuffed. He says, the lion doesn't mean as much to me as you think it does.

After the death of the lion, there is no need for Llewellyn to keep watch, I say. He doesn't have to hitch a ride anymore, doesn't need to take his turn at the ticket booth, the fire watch. We can let him go, I say.

And they say, but his eyes still burn in the fire.

But glass is a dead material, I say.

And they say, you cannot take him. He is us and we keep him alive and he belongs here and here and here and here.

But you don't need his body for that to be true, I say. And I pick up the scaffold of what was once Llewellyn and throw him over my head. And in the purple dark of the evening, I start running across the field. And the long grass pulls at my legs and makes them wet and cold and covers them in hitchhikers. And the sounds of the others chasing after pulls the air behind me. And those behind pelt me with beer bottles and beer cans and I keep running and shield myself with the frame of Llewellyn's body.

And I get to my truck and throw Llewellyn into the bed of it and climb in through the broken back window. And those behind say, wait. Say, wait. Say, we will come with you. We want to say goodbye. And I say, but this isn't meant to be goodbye, because nothing ever ends, there is no end, even when there appears to be. And I turn the truck over and pelt them with a rocket tail of gravel as I speed away in my truck. And they stop and stand behind as I leave, and there is fire shining in the tears of their eyes.

I drive to the Casselman, to the place Llewellyn laid his horses down and shot them. I drag the scaffold of his body down to the bank and lay him down on a spot I had cleared for him. I lay a blanket down across the skin stretched across the frame of him and cover it and kneel down and touch the warm earth beside him.

And I stand and pour a can of gasoline over what used to be Llewellyn and I light a match and touch that match to the other matches in the matchbook and let them bloom in my hand and drop the matchbook onto the blanket and watch the flame bloom across Llewellyn. His skin dries and cracks and, already turning to dust, blackens and curls off. Pieces of him float up and out over the water, brilliant for a second before blinking out. The wind carries him and blows him around, and some of the embers land on my skin and turn it to ash, too, and I can feel the pieces of Llewellyn's life burn into me—here pulling me up from the grass and wiping the dirt from my mouth, and here lifting me onto M&M for the first time, and here washing blood from my lower lip, and here showing me how to walk around the horse with my hand always touching the horse so the horse knows I am there and feels safe, and here plucking the strings of his guitar so Mom could cradle me into the warmth of the bonfire, and here showing Dad what I have learned about grooming the horses, and here squeezing the stump of Joe Joe's arm to stop the blood and save his life, and here and here and here and here.

I rub the remnants of him into my face and arms and hands when he is done burning, when all that is left is the cage of his body, when the last ember of his life blinks out over the black pull of the river. I take water from the river and cool him down so I can pick him up and carry him in my arms back up the hill and into the truck. I drive him back to the camp where they are all still waiting for me, their eyes cast into the dark. I stop in front of them, get out of the truck, open the tailgate and take him out of the flatbed and lay him at Rolfe's feet and say, this is all that is left. Say, Dad should be here.

Rolfe looks at his feet, the blackened and twisted cage of Llewellyn and says, what does this mean?

I don't know, I say.

Rolfe says, I'll take care of the rest. And make sure to wash your face or it will be stained forever.

I am watching the Ferris wheel spin and cleaning the grease from the inside of the windows when I see Sean stand and tip the bucket and leap out. When he lands he does not move. I run out of the trailer and run to him, push my way through the crowd that is forming around him. And I look down at his body and he is writhing on the ground, his right leg bent and broken beneath him, blood soaking through his jeans, down onto his bare feet. And he will not tell me why. And he will not tell me why. And he will not tell me why.

Don't look at it, look at me, I say. I can feel the bones move around inside of his leg, untethered from their other halves. They float around when he thrashes around. Don't move. Look at me. Look at me, I tell him.

I tell him, it'll be okay. I tell him, you'll have a souvenir from this day. You'll carry it in your leg the rest of your life, and whenever you feel it, feel it swell in the rain, feel it sing in that humidity, you'll remember the Tilt-a-Whirl, remember the Sizzler, remember the Ferris wheel and the decision to jump.

Don't worry, I say, it isn't so bad.

Don't look at the crowd, I say. They are just wondering why Superman fell out of the sky when he could have flown.

Did you want to know what it felt like to fall, Superman? Did you want to know what it felt like to be just a normal little boy for one second?

I turn to Rolfe, see him in the crowd. Get the splint, I tell him. It's in the office.

Give him room, I tell the crowd. Superman is going to be okay.

Quiet down, the crowd tells each other. They move back, make a theater of the ground.

This is nice, soft ground to land on, I say. I wish I could lie down in the grass with you. Hey, look at me. Right here. Right here. You think I can lie down on this grass for a little bit after and just look up at the sky? I like seeing the Ferris wheel from this angle. That's a long way down, isn't it?

Rolfe gives me the splint. I lift his leg soft and soft. Hey, hey, look at that cloud behind my shoulder, I say. I put the board around his leg. What shape is it?

A shark? Sean says.

A shark? Wow. Wish I could see it. I tighten the straps around his leg.

What do those clouds look like when you're flying up there at night, Superman?

He shakes his head from side to side.

Hey, hey, look right behind my shoulder. What else do you see? I tighten and tighten, feel the leg bend back into place. He shakes his head from side to side. What else do you see up there? I say.

An airplane, he breathes.

A siren cuts the air. I can hear it approaching.

An airplane, really? Are you faster than an airplane when you fly? I bet you are. I bet you are. I bet you're going to be even faster than a train when you run now that you've got this special splint on your leg. Did you know I flew once?

He shakes his head.

Yeah, I flew once. With the fireflies. Right over there in that grass. I remember spinning and spinning and then the air took me and I floated up into the dark and the fireflies caught me in their lights, and I floated there inside their lights until they blinked off and then I fell, too, but maybe not so far, maybe not as far as my man Superman could fall when he wanted. And I laid down in the grass just like you, down in the soft, soft grass and felt it cold against my skin. And the fireflies danced around me and they blinked their lights and blinked and blinked.

I tighten and tighten the straps. He thrashes his head.

Hey, hey, look at me, look at me. Yeah, I remember. I remember what it felt like to fly. I've tried to fly so many times since that night, so many times, but I always come back down. Isn't that weird? I always come back down.

I feel the leg bend back into shape. His face goes white and then slack and soft and quiet. A hand touches my shoulder. An EMT stands over me.

Good job, he tells me.

I stand up. Sweat is in my eyes. I wipe my face and smear Sean's blood across it. I carry his blood on my face and feel my own blood pound through my neck, my own blood still safe inside my hands, the hands I used to splint his bones back into shape. The yellow lights of the Ferris wheel flicker on.

Dad has always been a machine, but now he is part mechanical, too, but also flesh, maybe, for the first time, bone and blood and skin worn and tired and small as he steps into the trailer, his eyes a child's eyes, all the mad fierce blue burned almost white behind the glasses he wears now. We do not speak. He shuffles over to the silver bowl, all his familiar movements once liquid, full of power and concentration, now hitched, unsure, unsteady. He sees the mixture churning beneath my hands, squints, eyes the grain of the flour. I fill the fryers with oil, turn on the propane tanks and we switch positions. He holds his hands over the oil, feels the heat rising from it, makes an adjustment to the flame, holds his hands over the fryer again, watches the vapors snake around his hand, makes an adjustment to the flame.

The space is small. Our backs are pressed. I can feel sweat through his shirt, the tension in his back. He pours a tester. Too much water, pours too fast, he says. We switch again. He takes my mixture, combines it with water. Try this, he says. I pour the batter in a funnel, etch out an eight, close the circle. He eyes me over my shoulder. Nods. That's it, he says. In this way, with his memory, he returns.

It'll be nice to have the help again, he says.

You are assuming things that won't happen, I say.

You belong here.

I can belong in a lot of places.

Is this that New York bullshit?

We switch places again. He takes the funnel, flicks his wrist, etches out a half moon. Turns it over and over. Takes it out. Puts it on a plate. Try it, he says.

I pick up the dough with my fingers, feel the oil burn on my skin. I take a bite of the half moon, feel the crunch of the outside, the soft, soft center where the dough is on the edge of underdone. This one is perfect, I say.

He takes a bite, grunts, adjusts the flame.

The riderless Zipper lifts its cages into the sky. The Ferris wheel begins to turn. The Octopus lifts its arms and groans to life. Gamer's Alley begins its cadence. The lines begin to form. The window opens. I call the orders. The dough blooms in the oil. In this way, with our old routine, we return.

Dad is still nimble with his hands, but the balance of his work is off. He overextends, crashes into it all as though he were chasing himself. He takes over both sides of the work. The trailer shrinks. He expands inside of it. His face grows red. He sweats. His prosthetic leg swings and slams into the propane tanks, the mixing table, the supply closet, me. He burns inside of himself, stumbles around the floor of the trailer cursing the version of his body that ran in front of him.

You should take a break, I say.

I don't need one, he says. He wipes the sweat from his face with a towel. You belong here, he says.

You belong here, I say. It's not the same thing. And then I let it all out, because I am tired of playing this dance of burying everything unsaid beneath work and routine. I say, I will be here for the next three days until you find your balance again. And I say, I did this so you can stay with those who actually care, so you can continue to exist. And I say, but I'm too big to fit into the space you expect me to fit into.

Look at you, he says.

Yes, look at me, Dad. Look at me.

Go on if you want to. Go, he says.

I step out of the trailer. The sun pools just above the trees. I walk into a field, take my shoes off and push my feet into the grass. I can hear the bell of the strength tester ring and ring again. The smell of grease, burned sugar, fried dough, hamburger. I flex my toes into the grass, feel the blades rip between them.

I look out over the midway, the others moving around, their trailer doors open to the cool evening air, carrying in their supplies; prepping their apples on a table outside, rolling them in caramel and peanuts; filling containers of water from spigots attached to a barn. I can hear the shuffling of a broom. A girl rolls in the grass in front of me and stops, looks up, smiles and runs off, her bare feet a swish through the grass.

A sound pierces through, a deep cry pulled from the deepest parts of the body, ripped and raw and quaking, dragged up through the throat, louder and more desperate as it goes. I look back at Dad's trailer, at the sound vibrating through its open window, and run.

I open the door. Dad has his hands plunged into the hot

oil. His head is thrown back. His mouth is a black hole pulling in the entire universe. I run over to him, pull his hands out of the fryers, feel the hot oil burn pinpricks into my hands, arms, neck. His entire body is shaking. His hands and arms to mid-forearm are bone-white and leathery and crisp like the skin of a fried chicken. He is screaming. Everything is falling apart and shaking. He falls to his knees and yells, you want it, you can have it all. He slams his fists into the floor and the skin cracks and bursts open, exposes the bone underneath. Blood pools around his knees. His white eyes are galaxies behind his glasses.

I fill a bowl with water from a container, kneel down into his blood and grab his hands and plunge them deep into the bowl. His eyes roll back and he slumps backward and I can feel his weight pulling me back with him and I hold on to his arms tight and pull him forward and keep them submerged into the water, and his momentum swings forward and he slumps against me, his head crashing into my chest and I tell him, what did you do? What did you do? And his slack body traps me to the floor. And I hold onto his hands and push against his dead weight and scream, help me, help me, help me, help me, help me, help me. Joe Joe comes running in and looks down at Dad's blood and his slack body and his cooked hands. And I am still screaming. And he hooks my chin and pulls my eyes into his and says, what can I do? I freeze and I think and remember and say, there's gauze under the back sink in the kit. And he looks under the cabinet behind the sink and throws everything out—the Murphy's oil soap, the Comet, the steel wool, the paint scraper hit me as they go flying. And I yell, turn off the propane. And Joe Joe says, shit and runs over and turns off the propane and then scrambles back under the sink and finds the first aid kit and throws it to me and runs out of the trailer. I let my father down so he is lying on the floor, and I pull the gauze out and unroll it and cut two long pieces and plunge them into the water. I wrap them around Dad's hands and forearms and gather him up and lift him—he feels like a hollow box, like a small bundle of sticks in my hands. And I kick the door open and I step out of the trailer into the gold of the sun and the first cool breeze of the evening. And the faces of the carnival are all turned toward me. And I hold Dad bundled in the gauze close to my chest and I run and I run and I run.

The day after Dad returns to the hospital, this time for third degree burns on his hands and forearms, Joe Joe lets me control the Ferris wheel. I am spraying the floor of Dad's trailer with a hose, spraying the blood and skin out of the back door, when Joe Joe comes in. I look up.

The deadline has passed, I say.

What are you talking about?

I'm not going to leave, I say. I move the mop back and forth across the floor. I don't know what to do with this.

Fuck the trailer, he says. Come on. Joe Joe takes me over to the Ferris wheel, takes my hand and puts it on the control, says, today she is yours. Dad's blood pools on the floor, watery and pink, back in the trailer. I take the handle of the motor and pull the lever back and lurch the Ferris wheel into life and see the dangling feet swing out over the big blue expanse of the sky and see their feet kick out and swing the bucket back and forth when I pull the lever forward and let another three people on. And Joe Joe lifts the bar for them as they step in and they close the bar over their heads and I pull the lever back and I pull them into the sky, too. I can feel the power of the motor vibrate in my hands and I can feel the power of this motion that lifts these little feet, these little legs kicking out into the clouds, and I can see Mom putting her roses in her basket and walking out into the midway and I can see Dad's hands covered in pig skin and gauze and I can see the fireflies bloom yellow between my fingers and I can see the giant blue universe of Dad's eyes staring out from under the table and I can feel the rumble of M&M's throat when he nickers as I feed him from my hand in the stables in the purple dark of the morning and I can feel the rumble of the Ferris wheel lifting my riders higher and higher into the sky. I pull back on the lever and let go and let them roll around and around and rise and fall and swing out and back. And I do this again and again and again. The sun burns low on the horizon and Joe Joe turns on the lights and they flicker and burn yellow and red and white, and I pull the lever back and now I am lifting myself up into the sky, black this time, Mom by my side, the clasp sparking yellow in the incandescent light, and I pull and pull and pull down below and send myself as high as I can, high enough to look out over everything, up and up and up past the clouds and moon and stars and time. And there is Dad waving down below and there is Mom letting me go in the field and there is Llewellyn's body floating above the Cassel-man and there are the strawberry fields at dusk and there is the library and the sitting room and me with a pile of books and the motel rooms and my cracked hands and the diners and coffee and Jewel with her smile and her soft touch on my shoulder and the buses and the warm car rides in the rain and the pavement beneath my feet. And here is the carnival laid out and illuminated and beautiful and the people who walk wide-eyed and filled with the sweetness of it all and the children's squeals and the cadence of the games and the smell of oil and grease and sweat. And here is Papillon and its kitchen gleaming and silver in the morning and my station and the sous-chef feeding me blind from her hand and here is New York distant and impossible and welcoming in its hardness and concrete and steel and noise, its knowledge and possibility. And here I am rising and falling and falling and rising and falling and rising and rising and

After the last night, only Dad's trailer has been left untouched. Someone pulls down the last of the incandescent lights in the field and Rolfe and I stand in the dark in front of it. The moon rises at our backs and this is enough for us to see.

I have to put it in storage, I say. I don't know how long I'll be able to keep it.

This might be the last time any of us see it, he says.

He might not survive. If he does, they might not save his hands. If they do, he might not be able to use them anymore. I couldn't save him.

No one could save him, he says.

I don't know if that's true.

It does not feel right to do it in the dark, so I turn on the generator. The yellow Funnel Cakes sign illuminates our faces and the others come from their trucks and cars and trailers and RVs and they stand in the field with us and stand in silence around the lone trailer in the field. And watch the lights dance around the awning. This is our vigil. There is half a tank of gas left, so I hook it up to a fryer. I have a sack of flour and a mixing bowl. The smell of the oil blooms in the cabin. I fill the funnel and pour out four funnel cakes into the hot oil, watch the bubbles dance around their edges, spoon out the flyaways.

They come up one by one. The lights of the trailers illuminating their hands as I pass each of them a plate. And I pass and pass through the window the last of what I have until everyone circling around the glow of Dad's trailer has a plate in their hands. And I pull the fryer off the burners to let the oil cool and burn the rest of the propane off so the tanks will be empty and unwasted when I return them. I look out from behind the glass, but all I can see is myself reflected back at me, so I turn the lights of the interior off and look out at the crowd illuminated by the glow of the sign and the spotlights on the corners, and I watch them as they pull with their fingers great ropes of funnel cake from the edges of their plates, their mouths powdered white, licking gobs of caked confectioner's sugar from their hands. And I walk out of the back of the trailer and join them.

I see Sean on the edge of things walking on crutches, making divots in the soft earth of the field, the bottom of his cast caked in mud. I walk up to him with a warm plate in my hand and say, you can have mine.

You don't want it?

No. They aren't mine to keep anymore, I say. Say, do you know why this one is so special?

He shakes his head.

This one here that I am giving to you now, this one, you will find nothing but tenderness at the center.

He looks confused.

Don't you ever lose it, do you hear me?

Yes, sir.

And don't let anyone take it from you.

Okay, he says. And he hops away into the dark trying his best to keep the funnel cake at the center of his plate. I watch him stop at a dry place in the grass and dirt and mud of the field, toss his crutches to the side, pull from the center and smile.

When they are done, they come up to me to offer me their hands or their arms or their eyes or an arm raised in the air and then go, the tracers of their headlines scanning across the field before they disappear into the dark. Before he goes, Rolfe asks if he can help and I tell him that it is my job alone to do. And he nods and says, yes, okay.

I walk back to the trailer and go in. All the space that Mom and Dad used to take up is still there, but it is mine alone now to fill. I start to break everything down. This will be the last time I do this, breaking the trailer down, and I have to do this ritual alone, the ghosts of every other breaking down with me. I scrape out the fryers and polish the gas valves and wipe down the counters and scrub and mop the floors and clean out the grease traps and wipe down the windows and throw away all the empty and half-used bags of food and bottles of beer and clear out all of the cabinets. When I am done on the inside, I do the same thing to the outside. And when I am done wiping, scrubbing, and polishing the outside, I roll the awning up and turn out the lights and hitch the trailer to Dad's truck. I stand back and look out across the field. My hands vibrate from the work. In the east, the sky is already starting to turn gray. There is nothing left for me inside.

Some say darkness is the default human condition, that our morning coffee, its addiction, brewed from the same beans, in the same carafe, same filter, poured into the same five mug set, is an example of that darkness. Look down into your coffee mug, they say, what do you see?

I am drinking coffee, dark and pungent and earthy, from a paper cup when I sign the contract for a delivery van. When the salesmen asks what I plan on delivering, I tell him joy.

You're a strange cookie, aren't you? he says.

And I tell him cookies are not the kind of joy I'm talking about.

And he looks at me sideways and smiles beneath his oversized shirt and undersized tie. And I smile and shake his hand and walk away.

I have already walked away from New York, but I have not walked away from the kinds of cooking I want to do inside of my delivery van, so I cut two windows into its side, install a grill and a prep table and a refrigerator and a freezer and a magnetic wall for my knives, and I buy a folding chalkboard sign and I paint it the color of roses at dusk and I name it The Circle that Fits.

When I drive up, Rolfe and Joe Joe are waiting for me. And when they walk in and see my kitchen gleaming and silver in the morning light, Rolfe says, don't go classing up this place too much.

And I tell him, fuck that, and park and take my utility knife, feel its heft, feel the weight of it in my hand.

At some point in your life you will come to us: afraid that we will spin you too fast, launch you too high, drop you from too great a height, and in that hurtling lose yourself. And then the contents of your insides, kept there meticulously for so long, will fall out onto the dust and hay and gravel. But you will come and you will unravel in our light, on our carousel, our Ferris wheel, a goldfish in a plastic bag in your hand. And at some point you will stand, or have already stood, in our midway and be filled with our light, a pinprick in a universe of darkness, and be filled until the demarcation of what is inside will overwhelm the barriers that have kept it hidden, and you will come spilling out. Those who walk by you might consider you dumbstruck in your particular glassy-eyed half-smile meditative state, but in so being we are all dumbstruck.

This light is fleeting, they say—transient. And if we try to stretch this moment for too long, if our Ferris wheel is always available to you, always glittering in the darkness of your life, we would become routine ourselves, become your morning coffee, your afternoon tuna sandwich. So we must flee into the darkness so that we do not become a part of it, your routine, the circle of your everyday. We can only stay so long before we have to move on down the road, carry our light to the next town and the next.

This is our sacrifice for you: we will hold ourselves up to our perpetual light, dance with its flame, so that you may be, and in so being, dream. And here is Dad with his hands pink and scarred numb holding a television remote in his hands, and here is Mom passing her fantasies individually wrapped to parkgoers, and here is the sous-chef spooning brown butter over a filet, and here is Rolfe burying his face into the mane of the lion in the darkness, and here is Sean protecting the tenderness at the center of himself despite all the hardness around him, and here is the great lumbering hulk of the Ferris wheel ruling over the carnival, and here I am slicing my tomato, the memory of my hand moving left to right.

Contradictions Coexist
A Conversation with Kevin Lichty and James McNulty

Hey, Kevin! Thank you for taking the time to speak with me! We're so excited to be publishing *The Circle That Fits,* and I'm looking forward to diving into the behind-the-scenes of how this book came together!

I think the first element readers will notice when they pick up this novel is the rawness of the voice—the very heart-on-his-sleeve emotion of Daniel, first shown through a more nostalgic childhood lens, then as a more wary—yet still somewhat innocent—adult. Could you talk a little bit from a technical perspective of the difficulties in maintaining this rawness and emotion without falling into saccharine or melodrama?

Thank you so much!

So as Daniel's character developed, the thing I admired most about him was how much of a feeling person he is. He feels the world so deeply. And you're right, there is a danger in having that kind of a character at the center of your narrative. There are a couple of things that layer on top of and underneath how Daniel feels his way through the world. The first is his father, who tries to "protect" his son from those feelings by trying to help him build walls around those emotions. I think that's one of the central points of tension in the first part of this novella—that push-and-pull between Daniel's innate character and his father fighting against it.

There is also a reality that exists outside of Daniel's understanding, and I tried to show enough of that reality to balance against the emotional side of the equation. Without a narrator as a corrective, and because neither of his parents live in that reality, I had to use the other characters around

Daniel to help balance. Of course, what makes it really interesting is that all of the characters in this novella have their own tenuous connection to reality, or at the very least their own sort of warped perspective on what that reality is.

I like your method here of counterbalancing Daniel's more saccharine feelings with reality and the other characters. It highlights that the writing and the world aren't saccharine—just Daniel, the character. The push-and-pull of logic and emotion is always a lovely conflict, too—particularly as relating to the parent-child dynamic; I think of Malick's *Tree of Life*, where each parent is pulling their child in opposing directions. In that first third of *The Circle That Fits,* the father thinks he's serving his role well; as you said, he's trying to protect his son. These sorts of conflicts are often effective—simple yet nuanced.

By the end, both of the relationships end up becoming toxic for Daniel, and he makes a conscious decision to abandon them not unlike how they've both abandoned him in different ways (his mother literally, his father more metaphorically). What is there to say about familial relationships within *The Circle That Fits*?

Family relationships are a big, big part of this story. One question I kept in mind while writing was, "How does a person figure out who they are and how they should move through the world when those who society deems most responsible for helping them through that process are unable or unwilling to do it?" So I'd say in Daniel's case, the answer was the family he gathered around him as he went. Even if the relationship with his parents fell apart or became toxic, as you said, he still has a family and that family becomes much larger and more resilient even as he sheds past relationships.

In addition to the rawness, the moments of surrealism will also stick out to readers—and I think this surrealism often delivers the most surprising and interesting scenes in the work. I'm thinking of Llewellyn becoming taxidermy or Rolfe walking into his lion. What do you think these moments add to the story, and how do they relate to Daniel's narrative arc? Another, perhaps simpler, way of asking: what do these moments of surrealism add to the story?

I don't think those moments could exist any other way, especially Rolfe and Llewellyn and the lion and how their stories converge and diverge and who they are to Daniel. All of those moments to me are moments of transformation, of coming into or going out of one form of being and into another, and that's where surrealism lives: where anything is possible.

The novella is also punctuated by moments of extreme violence (Joe Joe's wrist, the lion attack, Sean's fall, and the father's oil burn—just to name a few). You mentioned earlier that these moments of reality help contrast Daniel's personality, which veers the novella away from becoming too saccharine. The narrative seems to have a deep love for binaries, often pitting two opposing things up against each other and parsing out the results.

Yeah, that's really interesting. I wasn't necessarily thinking about it that way when I was writing it, but I am also deeply interested in contradiction—not the kind of contradiction where they cancel each other out, but the kind where two opposing things coexist. Violence and beauty exist together (the lion is both beautiful and violent, for example). Safety and danger exist together (Daniel's father is both trying to protect his son and is also a danger to him). Softness and hardness. Warmth and coldness. So Daniel's deep emotional capacity and sometimes irrationally optimistic view (his softness) coexists with a hardness that's been forged by a deeply violent and toxic environment. He is both things at the same time.

So we've touched on the rawness and the moments of surrealism. Probably the third thing that'll be most present in readers minds is the language. *The Circle That Fits* is immediately and consistently lyrical. The right branching sentences and conjunctions—particularly those that begin sentences—carry you through the novella, and there's a strong love of repetition on display. Was it difficult to maintain this lyricism for the entire length of the novella? What were some of the difficulties, and what works did you take inspiration from?

A lot stems from jazz, actually. I relied a lot on what Wynton Marsalis, John Coltrane, and Charlie Parker taught me when I was drafting: how to layer meaning by going backwards in order to go forwards, how to listen, how to pay attention and be present in the moment. If you think about literary lyricism as a kind of music—repetition as guide tones, metaphors as chord substitutions, imagery as chord extensions, thematics as the chord progression underpinning all of it—you can take that raw material and riff inside of it.

There were definitely literary works I drew inspiration from as well. Michael Ondaatje's *Coming Through Slaughter* and *The Collected Works of Billie the Kid*. When I read those books, I could feel his sentences in my body, and I wanted to try to do that with this novella. Ondaatje stands behind me and side-eyes all of my sentences as I'm writing. Anthony Doerr's *All the Light You Cannot See* taught me how, if I paid attention, I could find beauty in stillness, and also how beauty and brutality live side-by-side. Christine Schutt's *Florida* is another one. So much of the power of Schutt's language is in what has been left out, the gaps between her sentences. But in those gaps, there is also something ever-present that vibrates beneath the words and pulls you forward. I had forgotten how much I was inspired by modernists until I took a modernism class in grad school and reread *As I Lay Dying* and got to Addie's chapter and felt the power of her voice when she finally is able to stand up and speak for herself, for us to experience her experience of motherhood. I was like, *yes, yes, this is what I'm after!* I return to that chapter often.

I'd say the hardest thing about maintaining the lyricism of the sentences was in re-entering Daniel's voice at the start of every day. I have to hear it. Once I was in it, I tried to be as present in the moment for as long as I could until the moment broke. Some of these vignettes were written in a single sitting, some of them took many days to pull together. It was slow going.

I can see the Faulkner inspiration in your writing; there's a love of stream of consciousness here. You mentioned the difficulty of re-entering Daniel's voice. Why do you think you have a difficult time dialing into the rawness of this character? What does it take for you to get into Daniel's headspace when you prepare to write, and is Daniel at all like yourself?

Daniel's emotionally-driven perspective of the world kind of stands in contrast to my intellectualizing of the world, so it's not a natural place for me to be in. In order to enter that space, I had to allow myself to *feel through* rather than *think throug*h what was going on the page—forget planning, forget thinking, forget strategizing. As a strategy (and I'm contradicting myself a little bit here: strategizing in order to forget strategizing), I kept a stack of index cards with the questions the story was asking on one side, and if an idea came to me for how to answer that question, I would write it on the other side. This helped me keep the story arc in mind while also helping me to see the shape of the emerging story. Without having to put my intellectual energy at the story arc level when I sat down to write, I could allow myself to enter into the immediacy of very specific moments and allow the emotional telling of the story to guide me.

And I'm going to contradict myself again here, because I also think there are pieces of me present in all of the characters in the book. What Daniel and I share the most is a sense of wonder and a deep appreciation for the beauty of even the simplest moments, even if maybe we process and experience these things in different ways.

Your contradictions here are appropriate, considering our conversation about opposites coexisting. I like your method of outlining the themes beforehand, then letting those themes guide you a little more naturally in the moment of writing. Writers can easily feel aimless, overwhelmed, or allow a story to wander if they don't do some form of outlining, as you have, before they sit down to write—whether that's mental outlining, gestating, or written tricks as you've done. Did you sit down to write the vignettes one at a time with a theme for each in mind? Talk to me a little more about the process of crafting a novel in vignettes.

I think my goals were more practical from day to day. They also shifted as I progressed through the drafting process. At the beginning, before I knew I had a book or that the arc of the story was longer than a few vignettes connected by a single narrator, my goals were focused around figuring out Daniel's way of telling stories, his cadences, his rhythms, so *play* was a big part of my day-to-day. Later, when I realized I was writing a story with a longer arc, I was really focused on the story and all the questions the story was asking. Once I realized where this story was going to begin, I realized there was a ton of leading information contained in what became the first vignette; that information begs certain questions. For instance, how does the relationship between Daniel and his father change, especially when the buffer between them disappears and Daniel has to take over the role of caretaker to his father? That became a central question for the first section of the book. But *play* was also always there. If you can't find joy in *play* and experimentation, it becomes very hard to come back every day when there's a lot of heavy emotional lifting happening or if the answers to story questions don't come so easily. *Play* is where a lot of the rhythmic and structural elements emerged. Daniel's voice, his way of telling, his way of seeing all emerged from *play*.

Back to the lyricism for a moment. There's a strong love of repetition in this novella. Could you talk to me a little about the strengths and weaknesses of heavy repetition? How do you decide when and how to temper it?

So, repetition to me is interesting. I don't think of it simply as a repeated structure—you know, like a monotonous banging on a drum—but also as a way of layering meaning. You can't take the context out of each individual utterance, which means that as something is repeated, there is a layering of contexts that piles on top of each new instance; so there is the singular instance that I'm reading right in front of me, but also there are all of the echoes that exist behind that instance—all of the times and all of those contexts I encountered that word, phrase, or image, that reverberate throughout the layering of the repetition. So you get all of those contexts emerging through.

The other way I think about repetition is as *guide tones* that help navigate the storytelling. Think of a guide tone as the root note in a musical chord—the dominant tone you hear as a chord is struck. As the sentence continues, I have to make sure to hit the guide tones along the way so that no matter how the sentence moves, no matter where it goes, there is always that tone that keeps it anchored.

How I decide when to use it and when to temper it has a lot to do with intuition. When I'm generating, I'm chasing what I'm hearing: *what is the music of this line, this phrase, this image, this sentence?* I allow that music in my head to just go onto the page. But I'm also trying to keep all of the practical considerations (like plot, character, setting, and motivation) in balance. So this is where revision helps—when you lean on certain tendencies during the drafting phase a little too much!

What did the revisions process consist of for *The Circle That Fits*? Share with the readers a little about what was cut or added in the process of revision.

The first thing I had to do was make sure all of the major questions were answered. When a story is told in this way, with vignettes that are focused on very small, very intense moments, there has to be a certain tolerance for gaps. There is a lot that happens off the page, a lot of years that pass from beginning to end, but that tolerance has a limit, too. That was the first task. If there was one thing that I cut at this point, it was how Daniel discovered where he was born. Ultimately, I didn't think that information was really necessary (and it didn't feel important for Daniel to tell that part of his story). One thing that was added to the initial draft? How Daniel discovered his father was in the hospital. This seemed critical for Daniel (it became part of the circle that he had to make fit), but also for the reader

At the sentence level, I had to find a way to balance the lyrical with traditional information delivery. There was a real skepticism in the sentences, which wanted to bend toward the lyrical and resisted giving certain expository information in a straightforward way. This was also about tolerance. How far could a sentence be pushed? How far did a sentence need to be dialed back? I wanted to make sure the story was grounded in some ways without losing Daniel's subjective experience of the world completely. Working with the *Driftwood* editors helped me see areas, especially in the final third, where the story got too caught up in Daniel's narrow lens and the outside world needed to be let in a little more.

The novella is very much inside Daniel's head—to the point where it often excludes exteriority (descriptions and actions). Could you talk a little about being so *within* a character and what that affords you as a writer? How does it limit you?

Being immersed in Daniel's perspective allowed me to move into and out of experiencing, perceiving, feeling, remembering, imagining, and fantasizing without having to really worry about if it was "real" or not, because all of those levels of experiencing and processing are real. There is a whole universe locked up inside of us where our consciousness and subconsciousness create our perceived reality together that a more objective lens might not notice. For a story like this—one where a character's experience of the world and their attempts at figuring out how to move through it and what their place is within it is at the center—the freedom to move between all of these modes of consciousness was critical to creating something close to the truth.

I would say the biggest limitation (or maybe the *biggest challenge*) brought by being this subjectively close to a character is the constraint on world building—on delivering information to the reader. There are obviously large gaps in what Daniel knows. This was particularly challenging when it came to characterizing what his relationship with his parents was truly like. We only have a child's perception and experience to guide us through that complexity. Also, what Daniel might think of as self-evident or routine might be something entirely opaque to the reader. I had to find some kind of a balance, because I didn't want to break the spell of the voice, but I also didn't want to completely disorient the reader.

I love the structure of this book. The vignettes are the perfect length, and they always keep the plot momentum moving while never losing the cohesive throughline of the narrative. The three-part structure also gives more cohesion to the vignette style. Could you talk a little about how and why you landed on the vignette and three-part structure? Did this take a lot of workshopping to figure out, or did the structuring and pace come naturally?

The vignette structure was there from the beginning. It actually started as a one-off. I didn't realize it was going to be a book at the beginning. Once I wrote that first vignette, I fell in love with Daniel and those who surrounded him and his world, so I continued to dip my toe back into those waters; and every time I did, questions began to be raised that I felt needed to be answered, so I kept answering those questions. That's when I realized I was writing a book. The three-part structure came much later in the process. Once I realized what Daniel wanted and why he was telling his story, the book's shape started to emerge. And because of the closeness and immediacy (there isn't much of a reflective distance—Daniel is still close to these events, still trying to figure things out at the end), it didn't make sense for the narrative to have a smooth telling or traditional chapters, but instead to have these fragments of story and memory that emerge and then explode on the page.

I imagine and hope most readers will be emotionally invested in Daniel's story here; *The Circle That Fits* is an emotional journey told with tenderness and lyricism. Is there anything you'd like to say to readers who see themselves in Daniel and his plight?

For a long time, I was writing for myself. I fell in love with these characters and this world, and I am deeply honored to have the chance to share them with others and to have this story resonate with even a single person. I hope anyone who sees themselves in Daniel finds hope here the way I did when I got to the end. Daniel figured some things out. There's still a lot of things for him to figure out, but I see a future with more agency and beauty for him when he's ready.

Acknowledgments & Thank You

I am eternally grateful to the editors and readers who saw early value in the vignettes and fragments contained here and have published portions of this text in their pages in various forms, including: *Four Chambers Press* under the titles "I Dream of Candy Apple and Blood," "Llewellyn's Marble Eyes," and "Between a Minivan and a Stationwagon"; *Palooka Magazine* under the titles "Invention of a Galaxy," "The Closeness of Everything," and "Their Velvet Lips"; *Ponder Review* under the title "The Space Between"; and *Yemasee* under the title "Fire Watch." Without their support and encouragement, I may never have seen this project through.

A special thank you, too, to those who helped, encouraged, or inspired me to continue writing this book. To Beckian Goldberg, who showed me how story can be poetry and poetry can be story and that there need be no division between the two. To Matt Bell, in whose class on acoustics the first vignette appeared as an experiment. To Alberto Ríos, who showed me how to play Jazz with language. To T.M. McNally and Tara Ison who encouraged me during my early drafts. To Jenny Irish who encouraged me in late drafting. Finally, to my cohort of Kathryn Bucolo, Megan Granata, María Álvarez, and Aria Curtis who taught me so much about writing, who I was in awe of every day, and who inspired me to become better and worthy enough to sit in the same workshops with.

Kevin Lichty was born and raised in the Virginia suburbs of Washington, DC. He received an MFA in Fiction from Arizona State University where he teaches composition. His work has appeared in *Yemasee, Ponder Review, Palooka, Broad River Review,* and elsewhere.

Printed in the USA
CPSIA information can be obtained
at www.ICGtesting.com
JSHW021936291023
50810JS00008B/51